Lost For Christmas

Copyright

First Edition, February 2025

Paperback ISBN: 978-1-961966-83-3

Published by: Carxander Publishing
Wisconsin

Dedication

To the shy, submissive hearts who need a dominant man and a hand necklace to stay centered and sane.

Opening Quote

Lay your body on the altar. Let the gods bear witness when I carve my name into your skin like scriptures. If they wanted you holy, they should've chained you tight, but they left you in my arms on a godless night. Your breath drips sin, your thighs burn lust. Every gasp, every scream, got me drunk on your trust. You told me, "Damn the world, just don't leave me behind." So, I set it all ablaze just to make you mine. I'd kill for you. Fuck you in the wreckage. Drag you down with me. Make you beg for the ending. Nails in my back like a sinner's prayer. If the world falls first, I don't fuckin' care.

Sins to Sacrifice by Az Apathy

Chapter One

"Tank! Pick up adds!" our team lead commands in our ears over our headsets. His voice is deep and does things to me that it shouldn't. It's calm as hell, even though there's no question in that dominance.

I watch as the second tank, the team lead is the first, of our ten man team spins into action "On it, BloodKnight!" TraumaBull says. His voice is also deep and dominant. It constantly sends shivers down my spine and hardens… things. TraumaBull, a Paladin Wogen, spins and starts drawing all of the additional enemies that have spawned.

World Of Warcraft is one of my favorite games to play. I probably spend way too much time with it, but it's a great stress reliever. My character is a Restorative Druid Draenei. I'm a healer who can take on any form. My favorite is a bat. I can heal the group, myself, and my Tank, BloodKnight. One of two objects of every fantasy I've ever had. The reason for all my wet dreams and morning wood.

And I don't even know what either he or TraumaBull looks like in real life.

I'm in love with a fucking Night Elf and a Paladin Wogen. TraumaBull looks like a very well armored werewolf. An exquisite creature that exudes power. BloodKnight is a Death Knight who is the most beautiful being, even though he looks like he walked through the depths of hell and took on the devil himself.

And won.

Both BloodKnight's and TraumaBull's armor is as intricate as the weapons they wield. It effortlessly fits their dominance. Anyone who looks at their characters knows that the men behind them are just as powerful as their characters look.

"Fuck!" BloodKnight grabs my attention. "Big heals on Tanks!"

I shake myself out of my inappropriate thoughts and focus on my Tank. "Got you," I say as I start my heal on BloodKnight. I notice that my DPS's are also low on health and quickly heal them as a group.

"Thank you for catching the group, MoonFire," BloodKnight praises.

I shiver. "You know I got you." I can't hide the grin, and I know it comes out in my voice.

"Dammit! Dammit!" one of our Hunters yells. "Taking aggro! Taking aggro!"

"Pop your cool down!" BloodKnight commands TraumaBull.

"I can't! DPS limbs!" TraumaBull barks, trying to get our Hunters and Warriors to take on Deathwing's limbs that are currently flailing all over the place and causing major damage to BloodKnight and TraumaBull.

"Get these guys off me!" the Hunter yells.

"I'm trying!" BloodKnight barks. "Where's our Priest? Why the fuck aren't you healing TraumaBull?"

"I'm trying to help Nems!"the Priest says.

"That's not your job! Heal your Tank!"

"Taking too much damage!" the Priest barks.

"We're in Phase Three! All of my heals are going to the group and my Tank! Heal your damn Tank!" I yell, throwing as much of my power at TraumaBull as I can to keep him alive. He's not my Tank, but I'll do whatever I can for him. My spells are disappearing fast. "We're already down a fucking Healer because of you!" I yell at the Priest.

"Tentacles!" TraumaBull yells. "God fucking dammit! DPS! Limbs! I can't fucking take adds and limbs!"

There's a flurry of action, but it's no use. Everyone is running around doing things they shouldn't be. The other healer, the Priest, whose sole job is to heal TraumaBull while I focus on the group and BloodKnight, isn't doing his job. What we have is chaos, and a fucking Priest acting like a damn Hunter.

"No! No! No! Dammit! Too much damage! I can't keep up with the group and my Tank!" I yell as my fingers fly across my keys. I throw all I have left at BloodKnight and Traumabull, but there's nothing left for the group. "I can't keep up with both Tanks and the group!"

"That's because you're the only fucking one healing! Dammit!" BloodKnight yells.

Deathwing, the boss we're fighting, is all over the place and everywhere else. There are too many adds. Too much aggro. The tentacles are moving too fast. It doesn't matter what any of us do, even if we have the upper hand for a second, Deathwing recovers far too quickly. Everyone takes way too much damage.

When it's finally over, it's an embarrassing loss for us.

No one says a word.

All anyone else can hear is breathing. Someone is panting. I stare at the screen in disbelief. I don't know how we started so well only to end up taking that hard of a loss.

The silence is deafening.

"Well, that's a wipe," BloodKnight growls as he takes a deep breath. "Pope, what the fuck, man?"

"I'm used to being a Hunter, man. Fuck this Priest bullshit," Pope grumbles. I bite my lip because I know what's coming next.

"Then, why the fuck did you play Priest this run, asshole?" Nems cuts in. He's one of the best Hunters we have, and Pope made him look like shit out there. I lean back in my chair and cross my arms over my chest. This is about to get good.

"Because you fucking needed a third healer! That's why!"

"Lotta good it did, mate," our Australian, Lachlan, growls, his accent heavier when he's pissed, which he obviously is. "I was fuckin' takin' aggro, and I'm not a fuckin' Hunter, righ', mate?"

He's right. He's not a Hunter. He's not a Tank. He's literally not a player who should've been taking on any damage at all. He's the fucking Shaman. He was supposed to be able to save us all in that third phase.

Instead, he died at the beginning of Phase Three because fucking Pope decided to go off and be a Hunter.

"There are a lot of issues we need to work through before we go back against Deathwing," Pope says calmly.

"Like all the fucking problems weren't on you, man." I've been quiet, but he's the reason we lost that battle, and he needs to be aware of it.

"Oh fuck off," Pope growls.

"Don't fucking tell him to fuck off, man," BloodKnight says, his voice dropping to a dangerous and protective level that makes things harden that shouldn't.

"It's not his fucking fault we lost. He gave everything he had out there," TraumaBull agrees, his voice just as dark and protective as BloodKnight's.

"If it weren't for him, we'd have lost that battle in Phase Two," BloodKnight continues. "I told you many times to pull the fuck back. We lost our Shaman because he was taking on damage he fucking shouldn't have, dude."

"What the hell was I supposed to do? Nems -"

"Was fine!" TraumaBull yells. Finally breaking his cool demeanor. "He was fine! He had all the help he needed! Until you went in and fucked everything up! You're a fucking Priest! Your sole job was to heal me! Instead, MoonFire suddenly became the only fucking healer out there and was trying to heal me, his Tank, and the whole fucking group! That's why we have three healers! One for me! One for BloodKnight! And one for the fucking group! Who you got killed!"

"I didn't get him fucking killed, you fucking prick! I was -"

"Helping Nems!" BloodKnight barks. "Yeah! So you keep saying, but it wasn't your fucking job! We went into that with our assignments. Yours was to focus completely on TraumaBull. You're a fucking new healer. I didn't want you doing too much. That's why I had MoonFire healing me and helping out with the group! So your focus could be completely on your Tank! You're not a fucking Hunter!"

"You think you're right all the time! I fucking hate running with you, dude," Pope says. "You're lucky I don't know you in real life. I'd beat your fucking ass."

There's a chorus of laughter, including my own.

"Oh yeah?" BloodKnight says. I can hear both the danger and smirk in his voice and imagine he's giving the screen a half smile while he folds his arms over his chest, much like what I'm doing right now. "How 'bout I shoot you my address, and you come make good on that threat, huh? Bet you don't walk out with both fucking legs." His Southern accent drips venom.

"Tough guy, huh?" Pope says, cockiness exuding through the headset.

TraumaBull laughs even harder. "Dude, you have no fucking clue."

"I'm not going to sit here and -"

"You're right," BloodKnight says, effectively cutting Pope and his bullshit off. "You're not going to sit here. Not with us. You're out."

And with that, BloodKnight kicks Pope out of our guild. I let out a near silent moan that I cover with a cough at his dominant 'don't fuck with me' tone.

Once again, there's silence before TraumaBull sighs. "I'm fucking tired. I'm out, guys." My heart sinks, sad that he's not going to stay on longer.

There's a chorus of 'goodnights' as people start dropping off one by one until the only people who are left in our Discord chat are me and BloodKnight.

After a few moments of uncomfortable silence, I finally let out a sigh as I rub my head. "That was a little fucked, huh?"

"Man, you're not wrong. Who brought him into our guild? He just messaged me and told me die of ass cancer."

I can't help but laugh. Hard and uncontrollably. Every time I hear BloodKnight chuckle, it makes me laugh more. Like all of the stress from our run fades away as each moment passes.

When I finally stop, I grin and kick my feet up on my desk. "You did a great job calling. We would've had that if not for Pope."

"Yeah, we need to find us a new Priest."

"I know a girl. She works with me. She quit playing because she didn't have a guild that she clicked with. I didn't say anything to her about our team, but maybe she'll be a good fit."

"Bring her in. I'm down if she wants to try us out."

"I'll talk to her tomorrow."

Another silence falls upon us, but this one is filled with tension. Sexual tension that's radiating fully off me.

I reach down and adjust my raging hard cock, giving it a little squeeze. Between him and TraumaBull, my dick is so hard. I need to hang up this call and take care of myself before I do something embarrassing that he can hear.

And I need to stop thinking of them that way. The thoughts are wrong.

"Stop touching yourself," BloodKnight growls, his voice raspy and demanding.

I immediately stop and stare wide-eyed at my webcam. *Do I have it on?* I do a thorough check, my hand frozen above my cock. *How did he know?*

"Uh…" A sound I don't recognize leaves my lips.

"You think a dom doesn't know what his sub needs?"

I nearly choke.

No.

Correction.

I do choke.

On my own fucking spit.

"What?" I manage to get out, only after taking several deep breaths. His sub?

No, no, no. Not again. Not about another man.

"Are you going to try and deny you're my sub?" That smirk again. I can hear it in his words.

"I…" I trail off because I don't know what the fuck to even say right now. I don't move an inch. I can't. I have to be dreaming. It's the only explanation. There's no way he just called me his sub, even though that's all I want. Just to be his.

And TraumaBull's.

Oh god, no. I can't think this way about men.

"You…" I clear my throat and blink a few times, still not convinced he can't see me somehow. I look around my room. There has to be a hidden camera. Has to be. "Can… you… see me?" I ask.

I'm not even afraid to find something hidden. It's exhilarating thinking he might actually be able to see me.

It's just the fact that this is all happening, and I don't know what to do about it. I'm convinced it's not real. It can't be. Do dreams count as bad thoughts?

BloodKnight chuckles. "No. You can quit looking for hidden cameras now."

I pause again, my hand finally falling to my lap as I focus back on the screen. "How did you know I was looking for hidden cameras?"

"I told you. A dom knows his sub. Besides, if I wanted to hide cameras, you'd never know I was in your house, let alone where to look for them."

I let out a long breath and close my eyes. "Why do I actually believe that?"

There's a pause. "Because you know it's true." His voice is lower, almost a whisper, but so much more.

A hint of danger…

I let out a breath. "I'm dreaming." I have to be. Dreams are just that. Dreams. Not bad thoughts.

Right?

"You're not. I'll prove it. Reach down and touch yourself."

My body obeys, even though my mind is struggling to decide if this is reality or fantasy. Even though I know this is more than wrong. I'm going to be punished.

When my hand meets my cock, though, I don't give a single fuck. Every thought but BloodKnight and how good it feels touching myself disappears from my mind. I close my eyes and let out a moan. I'm so fucking hard, I could rip the seam of my sweats. I'm already sporting a nice tent. I'm not a small guy by any means, but he somehow makes my eight inch cock seem a lot longer, thicker, and harder than it's ever been in my life. I'm like the hardest of all stones. TraumaBull is at the back of my mind, how wrong this feels is sitting right next to him. I can hardly see him, hardly focus on the wrongness, because all I can think of is BloodKnight.

"Fuck…" I let my head fall back. I don't grip my length because he hasn't said to yet, but I don't think I even need to. I'm so close to coming that all he'd need to do is say the words. My sweats would be soaked.

"Good boy," he rumbles. "Now take it out. Slowly…"

"Mmm…" I do as I'm told like the good boy he just called me. My spine is already tingling from his words and my touch. I'm not lasting long.

"Grip it and stroke with me. Slow. Tease yourself."

My eyes widen. I gasp at the very thought of him touching his cock as he's directing me. Precome is already beading on my tip and dripping down my dick. My breath catches as I start stroking, using my own precome as lube but wishing like hell it was his spit.

"I…" I grunt and squeeze my eyes tighter. I can see him in my mind. I can't see his face, but he's tall. He's broody and dark. Muscular. He exudes sex from every pore.

My cock thickens. I squeeze it tighter because I need him to tell me when to come more than I need to release.

But not by much.

"Stroke faster."

"I'm so close…" I finally manage to rasp out.

"Hold on for me, baby. Let me get there with you."

I slow my own strokes down, but I can hear him through the headset. His moans are quiet, but he's really jamming on himself. If he's not using lube, then he's producing a lot of precome because he sounds wet as fuck.

I hiss through my teeth. I'm trying so hard not to let myself release, but the sounds of him are bringing me closer and closer to the edge of the mountain top I'm damn near about to careen off of. My hand is shaking. Chills are screaming through my body. If I could see myself, I don't doubt I look like a drug addict begging for his next fix.

I'm fucking trembling.

Sweating.

"BloodKnight, I can't hold on."

"You can. And will. Or I won't fucking let you come at all," he growls.

I suck in a breath. Every fiber of my being believes he'll make good on the threat, so I grit my teeth, squeezing my cock even harder in hopes that it'll help me.

It doesn't.

"Come. Now." BloodKnight grunts once more before he yells out.

"Ah!" I shout in just as much ecstasy as I can hear from him and black out. My load shoots up, covering the shirt I hadn't thought about taking off.

After several moments of panting for each other as we both come down from the high, my vision starts coming back. I'm dizzy.

"I need you to go clean up, babe. Grab some water. Get ready for bed. You can shower in the morning. You need rest. Don't let me catch you disobeying me. A dom always knows." His voice has dropped to a far more caring tone, while still holding that dominant edge.

"Yes, sir." My voice is raspy. Almost like I've been screaming all night at a concert, but I haven't. I'm just suddenly exhausted. I've never come so hard before.

So wrong. Punish yourself. That voice says to me.

"Leave the Discord open. I want to know you get in bed safe." Adam's voice cuts through my own and pushes it so far aside that for the first time in years, I can't hear it.

I nod as I get up and then realize he can't see me. "Yes, sir."

My legs feel shaky as they carry me to the bathroom. I do everything he said, following each command to a tee and doing them all in the order he told me to.

Once I'm finished, I'm even more tired. I walk back to my room and pick up my headset. "I'm done," I almost whisper as a yawn I can't control escapes my lips.

"Good boy. Now log out for me and get in bed."

"Yes, sir." I reach over and log myself out of Discord. I put my screen to sleep and my headphones on my chair before crawling into bed.

Once I'm under the covers, I swear I feel two sets of strong, warm arms envelop me, chasing the voices away. I close my eyes with a content smile on my face as I sink into the comfort.

Thinking of BloodKnight and TraumaBull holding me as I drift off has me feeling more serene than I've ever felt in my life.

Chapter Two

❄ Adrian ❄

"What's up, asshole?" Brax, or Nems, as he's known in the virtual world, says to me when he answers his phone.

"I was just going on a ride. Wanna come?"

"Hell yeah. I'm fucking amped and pissed at Pope."

"Me too. Fucker is out, though."

"He messaged me right after all that and told me I should've stuck up for him. Called me dick lover like it's a bad thing. I might like pussy, but I'm not condemning someone for liking dick."

"Dude is insane."

"I'll meet you at Buc-ees. I need gas."

"Yeah, me too. Give me five minutes."

"See ya when ya get there."

I laugh. "It's a fucking race now." I hang up and grin.

I quickly head to my garage and grab my helmet. I throw my wallet in my backpack, making sure my insurance and registration are in there. The cops in Texas love chasing bikers, but the ones in Piper Falls are on a whole other level. They have nothing to do. So, they chase us. It doesn't matter that we can hit over a hundred miles an hour, some way more than that. Piper Falls cops love the adrenaline rush they get from trying to catch us.

At least in my opinion.

Most of them are assholes.

Again… in my opinion.

Not long after I jump on my bike, I'm pulling into Buc-ees. "Fucking hell," I rumble, shaking my head. Brax is already there. I pull up behind him and tap my credit card against the screen so I can get my own gas.

Brax turns around with what I'm sure is a grin and flips the shield on his helmet up. I can tell he's grinning for sure by the crinkle in the corner of his eyes. "What's my prize?"

I laugh. "I'll buy you some chicken later."

"Done deal. Where do you want to ride?"

"I was thinking out towards that resort that burned down last year. They've been rebuilding. I really want to see how it all looks. I've seen some pics in the paper. It looks bigger and better than ever."

"Yeah, I saw a story on it the other day. They were showing some before and after photos. Huge fucking difference. Hard to believe just a year ago, it was all burned to the ground."

"Probably better to see it during the day, but fuck it. We can sit out there while the sun rises."

"I'm down. I tried calling Adam to see if he wanted to come, but he didn't answer."

I chuckle. I know exactly what he was doing. We were talking a few days ago about MoonFire. We both have a thing for that sexy voice. He sounds young, but he's a pro at playing his role and doing it better than anyone we've ever seen. He listens to orders. He doesn't talk back. And he fucking excels when he's given commands. We know he's over eighteen because we don't allow people in our guild if they're under. We ask direct questions, not just the standard 'are you over eighteen' type questions. We test people. Things like 'when did you graduate' are standard questions we ask. If they ask high school or college, we know they're a shoe in.

"He's probably out cold. Long day at his day job," I say, covering for him.

Brax laughs. "Long day bossing people around, you mean?"

I grin as I finish filling my tank. "Sounds like Adam."

"Did you know he just picked up the contract for the courthouse?"

"Dude. Did you forget I work with him?"

Brax laughs as we both hang up the nozzle. "Yeah, I forgot. Still a new development. You as a business owner seems all kinds of wrong."

It's my turn to laugh as we sync up our comms. He's not wrong. I'm thirty-eight and haven't held down a single job for longer than a year. Not that I didn't work. I worked hard at all of the jobs I had. I just always left for something better. Something higher paying.

And now, I don't need to work. My grandparents left me a fat inheritance a couple years ago. Cut my parents out because they were both fucking money obsessed assholes. I'm set for life. The only reason I work now at all is for something to do. I've worked most of my life, so when I didn't have to anymore, I just stopped. Being a business owner not only gives me something to do, it stretches out my inheritance even more. I'll retire and have plenty to live while still being able to give back and do all the things I love.

Like donate to the sportsbike club so we can help out more kids both learn how to ride, decide what they want to do, like dirt biking or just leisure shit, and help them get their motorcycle license. We also have money set aside for scholarships, buying Christmas presents for kids in need, and for the kids forgotten… teens.

So, being able to donate to something I think is such a good cause, keeping kids busy and out of trouble while giving them opportunities they might not have otherwise, is something very close to my heart. Especially since I know a good portion of my money will go to our Christmas event this year..

When Adam approached me about starting and running a restoration business, I was all over it. It's like a dream job. Not like. It is my dream. I've always loved working with my hands and building things, but something I've always been passionate about is history and keeping it alive and beautiful. Our courthouse is the oldest building in Piper Falls, but recently, it's been showing its age.

We're a young company. Neither of us have the best reputations around town, but our work speaks for itself. Neither of us thought we'd get the contract, but Adam pulled some fucking flying miracle out of his ass.

The city gave us the contract, and while we were able to undercut other company's bids, it's still more money than we've ever seen for any of our jobs.

And it gave Adam enough money to hire the top family affairs attorney in the entire state. Not many people know about his past, just me and Brax, but he's about to rake his lying ex over the coals. I can't wait to bear witness.

I follow Brax out of the gas station parking lot. I love my bike, a Yamaha R7, but Brax's bike, an electric blue Yamaha R1, is something to drool over. I have my eyes on one now, but I can't bring myself to buy it because I'm attached to the one I have.

Once we reach the edge of town, we open our bikes up. Brax's bike is faster than mine, but I keep up with him easily. I know he's not going as fast as he can. He'd leave me in the dust if he did.

"Keep your eyes peeled for the five-oh!" I say to Brax. "Fuckers have been getting damn good at hiding."

"I love the chase!" Brax laughs and pops a wheelie, but puts it down almost immediately. "Oh shit. There's someone walking on the side of the road up ahead."

We both slow down. The closer we get, the more we realize the person is a girl. She looks behind her as she darts into the ditch and disappears into the long grass. Her sparkly pink backpack looks familiar.

"That's Raina!" I say a little too loudly as my heart speeds up. "I knew I recognized that backpack." I got it for her when she was twelve for her birthday. "What the fuck is she doing out here?"

"I don't know, man, but if we don't get her, Adam's gonna be pissed."

"He'll skin us both alive." I quickly pull over. "Raina!" I call. "It's Adrian!"

She pops up about twenty feet away from me right where the tall grass ends. "Adrian?"

"Me and Brax, honey. What are you doing out here? It's almost four in the morning."

"Uh…"

"Raina, come here. You're safe. You know you can talk to me."

"Uh… yeah… Um… just a second, Uncle Adrian." She practically disappears in the grass, but I see it moving, so I know she's coming towards me. "Just… promise you won't tell my mom," she whispers when she reaches me.

"I'd never tell her anything. I just don't want you running around in the dark out here. It's not safe. You don't know who's driving through."

She nods as I hand her my helmet. She puts it on, and I help her adjust the chin straps before fastening everything securely. I don't have an extra, but no way am I letting her on the back of my bike without it. I trust myself. I don't trust others.

I put the foot holders down and help her on the back of my bike. Like a pro, she puts her arms around my waist and palms against the gas tank. She learned well from all the rides she's been on with me and her father.

Brax takes off. I follow. I hear Raina talking but can't make out what she's saying. I glance back at her just as she taps my chest to get my attention.

"Uncle Nems says we're going to Kaasa's Diner," she says loudly so I can hear her. I nod.

The entire way back to town, Brax and I follow every road rule. We haven't seen any cops, which isn't normal in the slightest. The town is usually crawling with them. I don't know how many they have each shift, but it feels like way more than necessary. Or maybe they only have a few, and those few know how to spawn in.

Kaasa's is one of our favorite places to go. It's a twenty-four hour diner that has some incredible food. They serve breakfast all day and night. It's the perfect place to go when we go out for late night rides and work up an appetite or just want a cool down after the ride.

When we pull into the parking lot, I groan out loud as the smell of greasy goodness hits my nose. Steak and eggs with hashbrowns and a giant pancake. That's what I need. I'd kill for it if I had to. Thankfully, Kaasa's makes it all readily available. No lives need to be lost.

We park our bikes in the same parking space and get off. I help Raina out of the helmet and off the bike. She clutches the straps of her backpack as her eyes dart around.

"Raina, you're safe," I say low and reassuringly. "I'm not letting anyone take you."

"What if she called the police? Or what if she told her friends or something? What if they're all looking for me?" Tears fill her eyes.

I immediately hug her because I don't know what else to do. "Raina, I got you. You're safe with us. If anyone comes in here looking for you, you know we'll get you out of here. I know you haven't seen us in quite awhile, but nothing has changed." I feel her nod into my chest. "Now, we need to get you fed. And after that, we'll take you to your dad."

She looks up at me. "But he's not allowed to see me. The cops will take him, and I'll never see him again."

I raise an eyebrow. "Is that what Carmen has been telling you?"

She nods. "My mom said that if he comes near me ever again, the police will take him to jail. She said he'll never get out because she'll tell them he…" she trails off.

I glance at Brax. His eyes narrow as mine darken. I know what she's going to say. The fact that Carmen would even say that is preposterous. Her father would never assault her, let alone sexually. "She can say what she wants, Raina, but that would never fly. I swear that to you. Your dad has one hell of an attorney now. He's never stopped fighting for you."

She sniffles and nods as her arms drop to her sides as she looks down. She follows Brax into the diner. I stay behind her so she feels surrounded and safe. When we find a booth near the back, I let her slide inside before sitting next to her.

"Tell us what's going on, Raina," Brax starts.

Our menus come before she responds. We order coffee. Raina orders a Coke before burying her face in the menu. I know she doesn't want to tell us. Neither of us will make her, though we'd both like to know what made her run.

After we order, Raina takes a deep breath. "My mom… she… keeps having all of these men over at night. The last one, the one last night, he was really drunk. He was yelling at me. He grabbed at me, but I ran to my room and locked myself in. After that, all I heard was them… doing… things…"

I make a face and shake my head. "How long has that been going on?"

"Years…" Raina whispers, her gaze locked on her fingers in her lap. "After they were done, I started to fall asleep. I woke up to someone jiggling my door handle, trying to get in. I was still half asleep. I went to open the door. I thought it was my mom, but it wasn't. It was the man she had there that night. He grabbed me and pushed me into my room." She pauses and sniffles. Brax and I watch her intently, waiting for her to continue. My heart is about to beat out of my chest. She takes another shaky breath before continuing, her eyes never leaving her hands. "I screamed and kept screaming. I fought. Clawed. Hit. Kicked. I got him off and ran to my mom. I woke her up, but… she… didn't believe me… She accused me of seducing him…" She shrugs like it's no big deal. But it's a real fucking big deal. "She kicked me out."

"What? Kicked you out?" Brax asks in as much disbelief as I feel.

She shrugs again. "Yeah. And then when I was leaving… she started screaming at me to come back. I ran when she got into her car with the man."

"Did you recognize the man?" I ask.

She nods. "Her attorney," she whispers as our food comes.

She completely shuts down at that moment and digs into her food like she hasn't eaten in days. She wolfs down her pancakes and hashbrowns before I even half of mine gone. I glance at Brax, who is watching her just as I am, likely thinking the same thing. She looks thin. Way too skinny for a girl her age. She's sixteen now. She's nothing but skin covering bones, and not very well. I can see the outline of her ribs and hip bones through her shirt. Her cheekbones look sunken. The way she's eating, I know it's not an eating disorder. She looks malnourished. Like she's starving. Even her long, blond hair looks like it's thinning. I remember it being really thick. Hard to get a brush through without detangler.

It doesn't take her long to polish off her eggs, toast, and bacon. Once she's finished, she downs her Coke like it's water. I still have some hashbrowns and steak on my plate. Brax has most of a pancake. Without words, we give our plates to her. She doesn't hesitate to clean both.

"Still hungry?" I ask her casually.

She nods. "I haven't eaten very much the past few months," she admits. "My mom has been on a drug binge with her sex binge. She has a guy there every single night. Most of them give her a fix of whatever drug she's on. She pays with her own self."

"Fuck," Brax whispers as he flags down the server.

She orders another pancake and more bacon. When the server leaves, Raina lets out a breath. "I'm able to eat at school, but only because my boyfriend brings me food. He gives me snacks on the weekends and at night, but my mom knows and takes them from me. I told him to stop giving them to me at night, and he did, but my mom got really mad at me. I told him, so he started giving them to me again."

"What do you eat at lunch? Because you look incredibly malnourished, honey," I tell her.

She nods again. "I am… He's able to sneak me a sandwich and chips, usually. If his mom gives him something like leftovers, he gives that to me and eats the sandwich. Sometimes, he's able to grab me breakfast, but I've begged him not to tell anyone. I know if someone tries to interfere, she'll beat me. She has before. Or has one of her boyfriends do it…"

"Fuck," Brax says again, like it's the only word he's able to form through his shock. I don't blame him. I feel the same way.

When Raina's food comes, the server drops the bill for us after giving her a refill on her Coke. She digs right in.

"I just need the bathroom, Raina." I nudge her. "You gonna be okay for a minute? As soon as I'm out, I'll take you right to your dad's."

Raina nods. "Okay."

"You good if I pay this bill quick? I'll be right where you can see me the whole time," Brax says.

Raina nods again as she continues eating. We both get up. I head for the bathroom, everything she said weighing heavy on my heart, as Brax heads for the counter to pay. I had no idea that things were this bad. It makes me think that her father hasn't been sneaking to see her as I thought he was. If he were, there's no way he would've let this slide. He'd have seen right off how malnourished she looks. She eats nothing on the weekends and only one meal a day during the week. No growing person can live like that. Especially not a teenager still going through growth spurts.

Once I finish in the bathroom, my mind's made up. Restraining order or not, she belongs with her dad. I'll keep her with me if I have to, but she needs to be out of that environment. We need to figure this shit out and fast.

After I'm done, I start walking to the booth we were in. What I see makes me gasp. Brax is looking underneath the booth and around the restaurant.

Raina is nowhere to be found…

Chapter Three

Knock! Knock! Knock! Knock! Ding dong!

"Fuck off!" I rumble into my pillow after looking at my phone to see who it is through my Ring camera.

Knock! Knock! Knock! Knock! Ding dong!

"I said fuck off!" I bark into my phone.

"Get the fuck up! I can see you on your couch. Open the damn door! It's important."

"Back off, Adrian," I growl dangerously, hoping he can hear the venom my voice drips. It's too early for this shit, and I was having a really good dream about MoonFire. My dick is painfully hard.

"It's about Raina."

My head pops up, my hard on immediately deflates, and I glare at my front door. "What the fuck about her?"

"Your ex kicked her out on the street."

I growl as I push myself up. I stride to the front door and slam it open. Adrian is leaning against my house near my door with his arms folded across his chest.

The fucking hard on is back with a vengeance because like MoonFire, Adrian is often the subject of dirty dreams.

Speaking of jeans, he's dressed in dark ones and a black, long sleeve shirt. His white Yamaha R7 is parked in my driveway. He looks like he hasn't slept, I'm pretty sure he's wearing the same clothes as yesterday, but it's better than whatever the hell is going on with me. Just glancing at myself in the mirror I have hanging by the door has me wincing. My hair is disheveled. My black sweats are hung low on my hips, wrinkled, with one leg riding up my calf.

It doesn't matter how either of us look, though. He's always going to be sexy as hell with his light brown hair and silver eyes. I've had a crush on him for as long as I can remember, but I'll never tell him.

I sigh. My fucking ex.

The sole reason I decided to give into the part of myself I'd tried to hide my entire fucking life. I never married her. I kept hesitating. I believe now it was my instincts telling me to back the hell away. I didn't listen, but I'm grateful I never got tied down to her. I haven't been with another woman since her, and I have no desire to be. Fuck all that drama.

Besides my issues with her, I got my daughter out of the entire ordeal, and that's something I'll never regret. Even though when my ex and I broke up, the custody battle got brutal, I have never regretted Raina.

After our last custody hearing, though, I haven't heard from Carmen or Raina. Carmen got a restraining order against me the day before our hearing saying that I showed up to her house and threatened her. That I beat the fuck out of her and tried to take Raina. It was all completely unfounded, but she somehow got two judges to believe her, one of them being the one who granted the restraining order. The other was the judge who heard the custody hearing. The same judge we'd had every single time we've had a hearing.

I still snuck to see Raina after school until I got caught and threatened with jail. I knew I couldn't help Raina if I was behind bars, so I stayed away. I told Raina the last time I saw her that she could always count on me. I'd always be there for her no matter what.

"What did Carmen do? And how do you know about it?" I ask Adrian, TraumaBull when we're playing WOW. He's my best friend both in the dungeons and out of them. My right-hand man in life and fictional battlegrounds.

And one of my secret sexual fantasies.

"After the battle last night, I went for a ride because I was pissed. I took Nems with me. We saw a girl walking on the outskirts of town with a backpack on. We stopped to check on her. Saw it was Raina. Obviously, we asked her what was going on. She sat and talked to us. We took her to that twenty-four hour place, Kaasa's Diner. She looked hungry as fuck, man." He shakes his head. I can tell he's thinking about it, but I need to know what's happening with my daughter.

"Fuck, Adrian. What happened?" My heart is about to beat out of my chest and go for a run.

"She told us Carmen has been on a drug binge. Hasn't been feeding her. Bringing home lots of guys, a different one every single night. Pays them with sex. Raina's been eating one meal a day for months at school, but she's had nothing at all on the weekends. No breakfast, unless her boyfriend brings it. No dinner. Her boyfriend gives her snacks at night, but her mom takes them and eats them. She's lost a lot of weight, man."

"Fuck." I fold my arms over my bare chest as I lean against the doorframe. Adrian's eyes linger for a little too long. It has my stomach taking flight, but I quickly shake it off. There's no way he's looking at me the way I hope he is. "Why didn't she call me? She knows that no matter what bullshit her mom pulls, I'm gonna be here for her. Fucking restraining order or not."

"I asked that. She said she'd been trying to. But her mom found out and took her phone. She couldn't remember where you lived. She took her mom's phone, who has an old phone number or some shit for you. She tried calling it, and some old guy answered and yelled at her for bothering him during his lunch."

I close my eyes and pinch the bridge of my nose. "She had to have put in a fake number in hers and Raina's phone. I've had the same phone number for years. Where is she?"

"Good question. We were getting ready to leave the diner after she ate. We were going to bring her here. I went to the bathroom. Nems went to pay the bill. She took off. I came straight here after looking for her for an hour. I didn't call the cops because I know damn well where that'll lead."

I chuckle as I let my arms drop. "No cops this time." I turn and walk towards my bedroom, taking the stairs two at a time. I don't need to look to know that Adrian followed me into the house and closed the door. I know he's waiting for me to change and will happily be my ride or die to find Raina.

Even though I know exactly where she is. I can feel her.

I hurry back down the stairs and grab shoes. I quickly put them on before heading to my garage. My midnight black Kawasaki ZX10R is waiting for me. I grab my helmet and put it on. I secure it as I open my garage door. Moments later, Adrian and I are riding towards the outskirts of town. The black, long sleeve shirt I'm wearing is hot, but it's armored and will keep me safe in the unlikely event that I crash.

Once we hit the outskirts, I ignore the sixty-five mile and hour highway speed limit and gun my engine. It doesn't take long before I'm approaching a hundred. Adrian has no issues keeping up, but I know if I go much faster than one twenty-twenty five, he'll start to lag. His bike is powerful, just not as quick as mine.

"Where we goin'?" Adrian asks through our helmet comm system.

"When Raina was around five, I knew her mom and I weren't going to make it. And with all the lies she was spreading about me and saying in court under fucking oath, I had a pretty strong feeling I wasn't going to get any kind of custody at all. I fought for it."

"I remember. It was a bloodbath."

"Yep. I stepped back because I saw what it was doing to Raina. She was withdrawing. I didn't want my little girl doing that. So, I took the weekends I got. We went camping a lot. There was one special place I took her to all of the time. It's right next to Piper Falls River. Not too far away from town." I start to slow down. "I always told her if she ever needed me and couldn't get a hold of me, to go there. I'll know she's there because a dad can always sense his daughter."

Adrian chuckles. "That's where she was going."

I slow even further and make a turn onto a narrow, dirt road. I don't speed down it because I don't have far to go. She'll hear me coming and meet me as close to the road as she can. The place is hidden. She wouldn't be seen from the road. And if she climbs the big willow tree, like she's always loved to do, she wouldn't be seen from the ground either.

I pull the bike over. Adrian follows my lead. We both get off it and start hiking towards the river. It's about a half mile. When I don't see her at the halfway point, I start to worry. My engine would carry. She'd hear me.

"Raina?" I call, my voice drifting through the air. I don't hear an answer. I glance at Adrian. My silent look is all he needs. We both speed up.

"Raina!" Adrian yells.

There's no response, so we start running. I know she's here. I can feel it. She should answer me. She knows my voice. She's been hearing it her whole life, and while I haven't been allowed to see her for three years, she should still recognize it.

We stop in the clearing by the river, slightly out of breath. "Fuck," I whisper. My eyes are on the ground looking for anything and everything I can see that might lead me to where she is.

"How long has it been since you've talked to her?"

"Three years," I tell him. "But you knew that."

He shakes his head. "I didn't. I thought you were sneaking time in behind her mom's back."

"I was. Until the school caught me and called the police. Instead of meeting her after school, I was met by the cops. I was arrested for breaking the restraining order she has against me. Spent seventy-two hours in jail, but I told everyone that I was out of town. No one questioned it. Not even you. I didn't want my drama touching anyone else."

Adrian rolls his eyes. "You're an idiot. You should've told me she fucked you over like that on trumped up charges. Or Nems, at the very least. In case you forgot, he responded to the call the night she got that police report against you. His report gave details of the injuries and more details on why he believed they were fake."

"I didn't forget. I also didn't forget how that bitch got all that shit redacted because he's not an investigator and has no training to tell if her injuries were fake."

The second I hear her voice is the same moment I see small footprints stop at the willow tree. I look up as she's climbing down. "They weren't fake. One of her John's did it to her. I tried to tell the judge, but he didn't believe me because he was also someone getting favors from her."

I blink as my mouth falls open. "What the fuck?" That was something I didn't know. I didn't know anything about this multiple partner bullshit until Adrian told me what Raina said to him. I figured this was a new thing. Not something that had been going on for years.

Raina climbs the rest of the way down and throws herself in my arms, though she winces in pain. "She changed your number in my phone and in hers. I tried calling you so many times before someone finally answered. It was an older man who screamed at me about ruining his peace. I didn't know what to do or how to contact you. I tried coming here so many different times, but I always got caught sneaking out." She starts to sob into my shoulder as her fingernails dig in. I hug her as tightly as I can while also checking her for injuries. I don't know why she was limping, but I don't like it.

"Shh… you're safe now," I rumble soothingly. "I'm not letting her take you back. I have good money now. I just hired a hell of an attorney to take the case. She loves cutting through bullshit in cases like this."

"They'll make me go back!" she scream-sobs, hugging me tighter than a death grip.

"No. They won't," I promise, though it's a promise I don't know if I'll be able to keep. For the time being, I might have to send her back. I'll fight that with everything I am, but I want to do everything right so I'm the one who comes out on top this time.

"They will! They said if I tried to run away again, they'll take me to a home for bad kids!"

"Who told you that?" Adrian asks, his voice as dangerous as my thoughts.

"The school resources officer! He said I'm a troublemaker and troubled teens go to homes for bad kids! Then he said after I spent time there, he'd just take me back home anyway!" She cries even harder, and my heart shatters like glass as she breaks. "Please don't let them take me away, daddy! Please!"

"Raina. Listen to me. I'm not letting them take you anywhere. I promise you. I'll fucking hide you if I have to." Fuck doing the right thing. I'll do whatever I have to do to keep her safe. "I have a good attorney now. I have the money to fight her. I've been building a case. This will help that. I'll call her as soon as we get home."

It takes a few moments for her sobs to subside, but they finally do as she pulls away slightly. She looks at Adrian before her gaze falls to the ground. "I'm sorry I ran. I saw the guy who was at the house last night. I ducked out and ran. I wasn't sure I could really trust anyone. I should've known I could trust you."

"You haven't seen me in years, sweetheart. I don't blame you for taking off. I would've done the same thing. But we can talk about that later. Right now, we need to get you out of here."

We all turn to begin our trek to the road, but Raina limps and nearly falls as she hisses. I catch her and steady her, watching her closely. She's babying her ankle.

"What happened?" I kneel down. She uses my shoulder to steady herself as I examine her ankle.

"Nothing. I just slipped. It feels like a sprain."

"It's really swollen, sweetheart. We need to get you an x-ray," I tell her as I turn around so she can climb on my back.

"I can't go to the hospital! Dad, she'll find me!"

"I'll call Nems. He can meet us at your house," Adrian offers.

"See?" I crane my neck to look up at her and grin reassuringly. "We got this. Now climb on so we can get the hell out of here."

Her smile is watery. I know she's just as nervous as she is anxious. The unknown is just as scary as monsters under the bed. And she has so many unknowns going through her head right now. I don't even know how to ease them all.

I pick her up and piggyback her to my bike. She doesn't know it, but I'm already several steps ahead of her. I've already figured out where I'm stashing her. I'll have Nems help with her ankle. I'm calling my attorney immediately. She can set up a surprise inspection of my ex's house. I'm done playing games. We've already started building a case against her. It's just on the fast track now. Fuck these games. I'm done.

Once we get to the bikes, I swing my leg over and settle as Raina settles on the seat behind me. Adrian helps her with the extra helmet we brought. After she's secured, we take off. I feel a lot better knowing no one can see her face. It's less stress on me when we get back into town. Just in case someone is looking for her.

I don't completely relax, though, until we're back at my house and safely in the garage with the door closed. I get off the bike, leaving her on it. I help her get the helmet off as Adrian walks in the side door.

"Nems can't be here for a few hours, but he warned me that Lieutenant Andrews is on his way over here because she was reported missing."

"Fuck," I rumble as I turn to her, putting the helmet back on as Adrian does the same with his. "I need you to trust Adrian, Raina. Understand?"

She nods. "What's happening?"

"You can't be here, baby girl. Not until I can get temporary emergency custody of you. I have a plan, but I need you to trust me."

She nods again, more decisively. "I trust you."

Once I have her secured, Adrian piggybacks her to his bike. I keep watch as he quickly takes off, Raina holding tight to his waist.

The last thing I want to see is my little girl leaving me again, but I'd do anything I can to keep her safe. Including hiding her.

I'm already on the phone with my attorney. Elana Rivera is a cutthroat family attorney who eats cases like this for breakfast.

"Elana Rivera," she answers.

"It's Adam Damien."

"Mr. Damien, what can I do for you?"

"I don't have much time. The police are coming after me. Raina was kicked out last night after being assaulted and attempted sexually assaulted by one of Carmen's Johns. She's been on a drug binge for a while and brings home these dudes who give her drugs in exchange for sex. Raina hasn't been eating because there's no food. I don't know what's happening to the money I pay for child support, but I assume drugs. I have Raina with a friend. She ran to me. She's so fucking malnourished. She has to be around eighty pounds. She's a small girl, but not like that. Her ribs are protruding. Cheekbones sunk in."

"Don't tell them where she is. Don't say a damn word, Adam. I'll meet you at the police station. I'll have you out in less than an hour."

"I need her out of that house, Elana."

"Don't worry about it. We'll get her out."

"The judge we've had so far, she's given sexual favors to. I don't know who the fuck else she's been doing that with. For all I know, it's the whole damn town."

"Leave it to me. We'll get her out, but Adam, listen to me and listen closely. You can't have contact with her. Wherever you stashed her, tell them not to let the police in without a warrant if they show up there. I'll block the warrant for as long as I can, hopefully long enough to get an emergency hearing. How old is Raina now? Sixteen?"

"Yeah."

"She can make her own decision. We have that going for us. I'll get a doctor to meet me where you have her stashed, but you need to go straight home after you're released. I need the report from the doctor to go into evidence. Malnourishment is a child neglect charge for her."

I see a squad coming down my road.

"Cops are showing up."

"I'll meet you at the station."

She hangs up, and I watch Lieutenant Caden Andrews make his entrance. There's no love lost between the two of us. We've known each other a long time and have hated each other for just as long.

I watch as his tall, muscular frame drops from his truck. I've never known him to wear a uniform. Always jeans and a dress shirt. His badge always attached to his belt. Gun always at his hip. Two pairs of handcuffs and extra magazines. Caden is a damn good cop. One of the best.

He's just an asshole. Has been for the past twenty years. Ever since I broke up with one of his brothers. Guess I left him heartbroken, but if it's not right for me, I'm not wasting my time. I don't think it's fair to me or my partner.

I lean against my garage and watch him saunter his way towards me. I fold my arms over my chest. He's got the cocky cop walk down to a tee. Fucker just exudes arrogant dickhead. Which makes sense because that's just what he fucking is.

"Where's Raina, asshole?" Caden asks, fixing his glare on me.

I roll my eyes. "Don't know. Restraining order, remember?"

"I know you have her. Witnesses place you two together."

"Oh yeah? What witnesses?"

"Carmen. Said you picked her up last night around midnight."

I chuckle. “Come on. You gonna fucking tell me that you believed her? Did she have video proof?”

“Actually, yeah. She did.”

“Funny. Because I was here. Online. Wanna see my history? Talk to the people I was playing World of Warcraft with until three in the morning?”

Caden folds his arms over his chest, obviously attempting to intimidate me. “I’m gonna believe anything that anyone else says if it means I get to arrest your ass.”

“Careful, asshole. Your bias is showing.”

“I know you know where she is, Damien.”

I roll my eyes and finally stand up straight, letting my arms drop. “You can come back with a warrant, Lieutenant, but maybe you should quit wasting your time looking for her here and start trying to figure out why the fuck she ran away.”

“So, you have seen her. That breaks your restraining order. Put your hands behind your back.”

I laugh out loud at that. “Fuck off, Caden,” I spit out. “You know as well as I do that you can’t arrest me on a gut feeling. Find my daughter.”

“Look. Adam, I’m not playing games with you. You’re under arrest. I have you on video. You don’t want to admit it, that’s fine. You’re still under arrest for violating the OFP.”

I glare at him. He has me. He knows it as well as I do. Faked video or not, he has evidence I was at her house. “You know my attorney is going to have a field day with you.”

“I deal with attorneys all day. I’m not worried.”

Except I know he will be once he sees who my attorney is.

Chapter Four

"So? What do you think?" I ask Presley as I hand her a vanilla latte for a customer before turning to make the next drink on the screen.

"Hot vanilla latte for Shane?" she calls as she puts it on the pickup counter. She turns back to me and nods. "I'd like to. I miss playing in a guild."

"We just need a damn healer who actually heals. That's the biggest thing." I finish a smoothie and iced coffee. "I can't heal both Tanks and the entire group. I can either do both Tanks or the group. Or one Tank and the group. I don't care, but I can't do it all no matter how good I am.

"I definitely know and do my job. And I do it well." She turns to the counter once more. "Strawberry smoothie and large caramel iced coffee for Adelle?" she calls before turning back to me. "My biggest issue was being in guilds where everyone did their own thing and never stuck to what they were supposed to be doing. We had healers hunting. Tanks not doing anything. Hunters not taking adds and trying to fight the boss. No one listened to anyone. They just did what they wanted. I gave up finding a guild that actually works as a cohesive team."

"We definitely work as a team. We do our jobs. It was just that one issue we had. We booted him."

"I'd love to join. Just send me an invite. I'll text you my info."

"Sounds like a plan. We're excited to have you! I am, for sure. You sound fun to play with!" I grin as I hand her an iced hot chocolate with extra milk.

She makes a face. "It's chocolate milk. Why can't they just say chocolate milk?"

I laugh. "No clue. I don't even think this would taste remotely good."

"Iced hot chocolate for Jim!" Presley shouts as she sets it on the counter.

My eyes land on the door, my breath catching in my throat. I've been waiting all morning for the hot biker who comes in every single morning to show up today. He hasn't. Yet. He's here every single morning. He's the highlight of my day.

What greets me instead is another biker, hot biker's frequent companion, entering with a young looking girl. The guy is tall. He's a bit taller than me, but he seems taller because he's so much more muscular than me. I'm toned, but I don't look like that. I doubt he's spent a day in the gym, just like hot biker. His muscle tone seems as effortless as his walk.

I call him sexy biker. He and hot biker frequent my dreams as much as TraumaBull and BloodKnight. I've had dreams where all four of them have their way with me.

Something is definitely wrong with my psych. I need to see someone.

"Hey, Sloan," I say when he reaches the counter. It's the name he has us write on his cup. I don't know if it's his first or last, or maybe it's a nickname, but I love it either way. The girl's eyes are on her feet.

"Hey, Jake. Can I get a medium Oreo shake for my niece and a large Smores latte?"

"Comin' up!" I look up at the door once more.

Sloan chuckles. "Damien's tied up. Might be in later," he says, voice low. As if it's a secret just for me.

As I'm sure he intends, my face lights up. I nod and get to work on his order. I love working at the Cozy Bean Cafe. It's the first job I had. I got it at sixteen. I'm an assistant manager now. I've been here for five years.

But I've never had a crush like this. Days I don't see Damien and Sloane are horrible days for me. I look forward to them.

Secretly, it's because Damien sounds so much like BloodKnight. Sloan sounds a lot like TraumaBull. I've wondered if they are them, but I know that's crazy. The idea that they're that close to where I am is an insane thought. I'm not that lucky anyway. It would be amazing, though.

"Earth to Jake." Sloan's deep voice cuts through my impure thoughts. My eyes snap to his. I try not to melt, but it's not easy. He's looking at me like he wants to devour me, but the moment is broken when he clears his throat. "I think my order is done." He points to Presley.

She's standing next to me with a grin on her face as she holds the drinks. "For Sloan."

"Hate you," I mumble under my breath, hopeful that Sloan doesn't hear me.

"Love you!" she says as chipper and loudly as possible as she turns after I take the drinks.

I roll my eyes and turn back to Sloan. "Your drinks."

Sloan grins. "She sounds fun."

"She's a terrible friend. Don't let the innocent act fool you."

Sloan laughs a hearty laugh that makes my fucking heart sing. I will my dick to stay soft, but the traitor never listens. Thankfully, there's a counter between us so he can't see. I just need to be careful not to turn around.

I give Sloan his drinks. He takes them and winks as he and the girl leave. I groan under my breath and try to make my problem go away. Something is wrong with me. Two men? Fucking really? Why is this happening to me? There's no way this is a normal thing people go through.

I can't get either of them out of my head. It doesn't help that BloodKnight and TraumaBull are also sitting in there comfortably with no intention of exiting.

Fuck… me… My heart is in so much trouble.

❄❄❄

"Fuck," I grumble. I rapidly push buttons until my character moves.

"You okay?" TraumaBull asks over the private Discord we have with just the two of us and BloodKnight. He's been running daily tasks with me on WOW for the past hour. I keep failing.

"Yeah, I just…" I see something come at me from behind and can't counter in time. "Fuck!" I push my keyboard away from. Violently. Because that's how I fucking feel.

"Okay. What's going on, MoonFire? Talk to me."

I rub my head and take a deep breath. "It's been a long day. That's all."

"Well, when I saw -" He clears his throat and coughs. There's silence on the other end, but I can hear him drinking something.

"I think the question is, are you okay?"

"Yeah! Yeah. Good. Yeah. I'm fine. I'm fine." He coughs again. "I'm okay. Tell me about your day."

I narrow my eyes. It sounded like he was about to say something about seeing me. It makes me wonder where he saw me and how he knew it was me, but I don't push it. The tone of his voice when he told me to tell him about my day was extremely low, sexy, and dominant. It left no room for argument.

After a few moments of composing my thoughts, I take a deep breath. "I just had a rough day. I worked. No issues there. And then after, I went over to a friend's house. He's an older man. His name is Henry. He hasn't been feeling that great. He lives around me. I noticed his lawn was getting long. I offered to mow it. He was grateful. Since then, I visit him regularly. We play games. I've done some grocery shopping for him. Things he's needed done around the house. I've gotten pretty close to him. Today, he just… I don't know. He looked so worn down. He was quiet. I don't know what to make of it. I feel like he's nearing the end and coming to terms with it. I'm not ready to let him go, though. Not yet."

"Sounds like it's good you've been around." TraumaBull's voice is so soothing to me, but I know it can turn commanding on a dime. Either way, it's so sexy. I just want to curl up in it and let him do whatever he wants to me. He could reach into my chest and tear out my heart, and I'd simply say 'thank you' before I died.

I shake my head to rid myself of the thoughts. More punishment for my actions and thoughts today. "He's like a grandpa to me. I never got to meet mine. He died before I was born. Well, both of them died before I was born."

"I'm sorry to hear that. What about grandmas? Aunts? Uncles?"

I chuckle darkly. "I've been on my own since I was seventeen. My dad kicked me out because I came out. I'm proud of my sexuality. I'm trying to be proud of who I am. But I live in the Bible Belt. So I still struggle. Being gay is worse than committing adultery here. Which is interesting because my dad did that a lot."

"Being gay isn't a sin."

"According to him and my entire family, it is. I haven't spoken to any of them since that day. I got a lot of calls and texts condemning me for a while. I finally changed my number."

"Do they live around you? Or did you move?"

"They live around me. But I barely see them. They avoid me like the plague. Which is just fine with me. I'm better without them. After I left, I started seeing a lot of things that they had been doing my whole life. Manipulation was a big one, but there was a lot of religious abuse. Mental for sure. Emotional was the biggest one, though." I lean back in my gamer's chair completely giving up on the game for the night. I can't focus on it. There's a lot of stuff I'm leaving out. Stuff I'm not ready to talk about.

"You live in the Bible Belt, huh?" There's some shuffling on his end. I assume he's settling like I am.

"Yep. Most people where I am are pretty accepting, but there are a few crazies sprinkled in. Like my family. My parents and one grandmother live here. The rest are scattered throughout the Bible Belt. Some are in Texas. Some are in Louisiana. A few are in Kentucky. A lot of them ended up around Tennessee and South Carolina."

"So they're really scattered all over. Kinda surrounding you."

"Very much." There's a long pause, but it doesn't feel awkward. It's peaceful. Like I'm just sitting enjoying the love of my life's company. I shake my head again. I need to stop this fantasizing shit. It's not helpful or productive. It's harmful. "What about you?"

"Ah, not much to tell. My parents were money hungry assholes. I left the second I could. My grandmother was getting older. She was well off, but I did a lot to help her out. I never asked her for a time. I worked for everything I have. She appreciated that. When she died, I got everything. My parents are still bitter about that."

By the time he finishes, I'm grinning from ear to ear. "A real life hero. Helping out your grandmother so selflessly."

He laughs. "I'm far from a hero. More like an anti-hero. Like Deadpool. Sharp as fuck, quick witted, devil tongue. But he fights for those he loves and cares about, no matter how dirty. That's like me. A hero will save the world and leave those he loves behind for the greater good. That's not who I am."

I grin even wider. "I fucking love that. A protector on and off the screen."

We fall into that comfortable silence once more, and while I love that I feel that comfortable with him, it gives my mind time to wander into dangerous territory. Sloan and TraumaBull take me to the bed. They both have their way with me. Ever since I saw Sloan at the coffee shop today, I can't get him out of my head. TraumaBull sounds a lot like him. So much like him that I'm really struggling to believe they are separate people.

But I have to. I have zero evidence to say otherwise.

That's why I'm imagining them both. Man and beast.

I'm fucking insane. And need to be punished for those thoughts.

"Quit touching yourself without me." That dominant edge hits TraumaBull's voice, and it's at that moment that I not only realize I have my cock out and that I'm stroking it, but also that he, just like BloodKnight, knew what I was doing.

"How-"

"A dom knows." I hear more shuffling on his end as I freeze.

That's the same thing BloodKnight said to me.

Same words.

"I don't -"

"Don't think. Just stroke yourself with me. Start slow. Do you have lube?"

I glance at it. It's sitting on my desk. "Y-yeah…"

"Grab it. I want you to pour some over your cock."

I keep my grip on my shaft and reach for the lube. My heart races in my chest. I feel it pounding in my ears. My hand shakes as I grab the bottle. I flick the cap open with my thumb and take a shaky breath in a failed attempt to calm my nerves.

Is this considered cheating? Am I cheating on BloodKnight? Fuck, fuck, fuck! Why do I want them both this bad? So much punishment is coming at me tonight.

I feel powerless to stop what's happening, yet completely in control. It's so wrong, but I want it. I'll suffer the consequences later.

"Now, I want you to slowly rub that lube all over your cock and pretend it's my mouth. Warm and wet. Stroke all the way down to your base and all the way back up to your tip. Squeeze your tip like it's me sucking."

My breathing stops completely as I follow his commands. All the way down. The lube drips onto my balls like it's his spit.

All the way back up. I squeeze my tip and rotate my wrist thinking it's his tongue lavishing me. I let out a breathy moan when I remember that I need air.

"Breathe, baby. Enjoy it. Let your imagination go. Tell me what you want me to do with your dick."

"Stroke it faster," I saw without hesitation. "As you lick and suck that tip, taking me to the back of your throat."

"Fuck. Yes."

I hear what sounds like skin on skin from his end and realize he's stroking himself at my pace. I get really brave. "I want you to stroke yourself at the same pace you're sucking and stroking me." I don't feel very confident saying that. My voice isn't as strong as I wanted it to be when those words left my mouth, but they have the intended effect.

"Fuck. Good boy. Telling daddy what you need."

Oh hell…

Daddy…

Why does that sound so hot? Why does that turn me on so much? Why is my dick even harder?

"Mmm… daddy…" I try the words on and love how they fall so naturally from my lips. "I… I need to come!" I shout suddenly. There's no stopping it. I feel it start from deep within as my back tightens.

"Me too, baby. Come with me…"

The desperation intermingled with the sexy tone of his deep voice has come spurting from my cock like a volcano erupting. "Ah!" I shout. "TraumaBull, fuck!"

"MoonFire!" TraumaBull growls. I imagine his come mixing with mine on my dick and newly ruined shirt.

It takes us both several minutes to come down enough to move. I hear a squeak of his chair, and that somehow kicks my own body into motion. I haven't let go of my dick yet, even though it's soft in my hand.

"Fuck," I whisper, seeing the mess I made for the first time. "That was a lot of come."

"No shit. I got it up to my mouth, it was so damn powerful. I've never come like that."

I have. It was with BloodKnight, but I don't think it's a wise idea to say that. "I think I ruined my shirt."

TraumaBull laughs, a deep, throaty sound emanating from his throat. "Better go change, clean up, and get your sexy ass in bed. I'll wait."

"Yes, daddy," I say as I take my headphones off and toss them gently on my desk. I hurry to the bathroom to clean up. Once I'm finished, I nearly run back to my computer. I put my headphones back on. "Want to run those daily tasks now?"

"I do, but what I really want is you in bed. I know you need to be up early. You need your sleep."

"I'm wired."

"And you need to be unwired. Do your headphones reach to your bed?"

"Yeah. They're wireless."

"Good. I want you to lay down for me. Keep your headset on."

I furrow my brows but do what he says, though I'm confused about what he's getting at. "Okay. I'm laying down."

"I want you to think of my arms wrapped around you. Your back is to my chest. My mouth is against your neck as I hug you tight. Protectively and possessively. Close your eyes."

I let them fall closed. "Mmm…"

"Good boy. Goodnight, baby. Dream of me," he whispers.

And that's the last thing I hear before I'm lights out just as content as I was the night BloodKnight had his way with me.

Chapter Five

(Two Days Later)

I close my eyes and rub my temples as I lay on my couch. The past two days have been spent between sexual fantasies about MoonFire and Adam, and trying to keep Raina hidden. Fucking Lieutenant Andrews has been at my house four times, the last time was with a warrant. Thankfully, I was able to hide her at the Cozy Bean before they stormed my house. They hit me, Adam, and Nems all at once. I don't know how they managed to lump us all together, but I don't pretend to know shit about police work either. For all I know, it was an elaborate, corruptive scheme.

Or maybe he really is doing his job. I know there's no love lost between him and any of us. He'd look for any reason to haul us in, but actually doing it legally is more his route. The one thing I'll say for Caden Andrews is he's never been corrupt.

Which can only mean there's something huge going on right now. Something bigger than any of our comprehension. The question is what. What is it that has everyone running around like this?

"Uncle Adrian?" Raina's sweet, soft voice says to me.

I open one eye, but don't move. "Yeah? You okay?"

"Yeah… I've been thinking about school, though." She pauses as she chews her cheek. "I can't go, I know, but I need to stay caught up."

Fuck, I think to myself.

"So, I was thinking," she continues, "that I could have my boyfriend bring my homework to me?"

"Raina." I open both eyes as I shake my head and slowly sit up.

"He wouldn't tell anyone! I promise! He'd do anything to keep me away from my mom!"

"It's too risky. What if he's being followed? The cops would know he's with you. So they'd know that he'd try to see you or contact you."

"What if he contacted you?"

"What if they're tapping his phone? Or mine?"

She pauses and chews her lip furiously, tears threatening to fall. She wraps her arms around herself as she nods and walks silently towards my kitchen. I hate seeing her upset. I sigh before I stand.

"If we were really careful, I think I could see him," she says, turning back to me.

I shake my head. "It's too dangerous, Raina." I run my fingers through my hair as I think. After a few moments of her refusing to look at me as I pace, I finally make a decision. "I can't let you see him, sweetheart. It's too risky. He could be followed. His GPS could be being tracked. There're too many risks. But what if we have him give it to someone I know? Do you have any of his friend's numbers? Someone we can contact to get a message to him in person and not on the phone?"

She finally turns and looks up at me. "I could email his friend, Pierce. I have his email still from a school project we worked on."

"Does he check it?"

She nods. "He uses it all the time for school and stuff because he doesn't like giving out his number. I have his number now, but I didn't then. That was from a couple of years ago before I was dating Bentley."

"Okay. Email him. Tell him not to email you back. Tell him to go straight to Bentley. Not to call him. Not to text him. Just straight to

Bentley. Talk to him face to face. Tell him whatever you want to, but also make sure to tell him to grab your work. Tell him to drop it off after school today at Cozy Bean. Tell him to give it to Jake. He's the assistant manager. And create a different email. Like a throwaway."

"Okay." She quickly fires off an email with the fastest thumbs I've ever seen. Before I can even process it, she's looking up at me. "Done."

"Jesus. Did you already have a throwaway? You could be in a texting contest. Do they do those?"

She giggles. "Maybe I could win ten grand."

"Hands down you'd win."

"I'd beat everyone in seconds. And yes. I do have a throwaway. I made it when I thought my mom was snooping in my emails."

I grin at how smart she is before it falls a bit. "I'm really sorry you can't see Bentley or your dad right now."

She sighs. "I get it, though. I know my dad is working hard to make sure I end up with him. I don't want to jeopardize that."

"Good girl." I take out my phone. "I'm going to make that phone call, honey. Then I'll grab your stuff later for you."

"Okay. I'm going to take a nap. I didn't really get a lot of sleep last night."

"Okay, honey."

I watch her walk away before I grab my burner phone. It's how Adam and I communicate. Burner phones. I use it to call the Cozy Bean. I hope Jake is working today because he's my last hope at giving her a little bit of light in all of this drama.

"Cozy Bean. Jake speaking."

"Thank fuck," I rumble with a huge sigh.

"TraumaBull?" Jake whispers.

My heart simply quits beating as my eyes widen. "What?"

"Nothing! Nothing! I'm so sorry. What can I get for you?"

It takes me a full ten seconds to restart my fucking heart and start breathing again. TraumaBull? How the fuck does he know TraumaBull?

Unless…

No.

Nope.

That's not possible. It's not fucking possible.

"Hello?" Jake asks, I'm sure he's wondering if I'm still here.

Except he sounds like…

How the fuck is this possible? The coffee guy I have a crush on is MoonFire?

I clear my throat. I'll figure that out later. "It's Sloan, Jake. Listen. I need a favor." I rush on because I don't want him to get flustered and apologize again. I want to get off this phone so I can dissect how the fuck he guessed who I am. Or how he knew at all. There's only one option here, and I don't know how I feel about it.

"You got it. What's up?"

"This is a big thing, man. Damien's daughter. She's the one I came in with a couple days ago."

"Yeah, I remember."

"She's in trouble. Don't breathe a word of this, but he's working to get custody of her from her mom. It's a long story. I'm sure he'll tell you sometime, but I need you to keep this between us."

"Yeah. For sure. You got it."

"I don't know if the cops have come in with her picture or not. I have her. If they come in, tell them you haven't seen her. I have to have her boyfriend coming in today with her homework, provided he gets the message. Do you have caller ID?"

"Yeah, but it just says 'unknown caller'."

I give him the number. "Put it in your phone. Call me when he gets there. I'll be in to get her stuff. Don't tell him where she is. If the cops go to him, it's best that he knows nothing."

"Okay. I got it. I'll take care of it."

"One more thing, Jake."

"Yeah."

"You know nothing either. Understand?"

"I know nothing of what?"

I can hear the grin on his face through his words and laugh. "Exactly."

"You can count on me."

"Thanks, man. If there's anything I can do for you, just let me know."

"I will." Jake hangs up, and I practically flop onto my couch as I throw my phone onto the throw pillow.

"What the fuck?" I whisper. I lay my head back and close my eyes. "How could he know I'm TraumaBull unless he's in my guild? And if he's in my guild…"

It has to be MoonFire. It's the only thing that makes sense. MoonFire works at a coffee shop. He's said that. I've always thought Jake's voice sounded like MoonFire but talked myself out of it because I saw how he looked at me and Adam whenever we walked in. We both love flirting with him because he gets so flustered. Especially when we go in alone and one of us says something about him not worrying because the other one of us will be around shortly. It's like he can never quite figure out how we know he has a thing for us.

I'd never tell him or Adam, but I get a little jealous sometimes. I know Adam's sexuality. He's bisexual, though he leans a lot more towards men since everything that went down with Carmen. I haven't seen him with a woman since.

The issue is I've had the biggest thing for him for as long as I can remember. He was my first crush. He's the one I fantasized about. He still fucking is. Sometimes when I'm with someone else, I have to think of Adam just to finish.

I know that's not going to last forever. Pretty soon I won't be able to be with anyone else because it's Adam I've always wanted.

Until Jake came into the picture. He's the first person other than Adam that I've been able to think about and get off to.

Him and MoonFire.

I lay back down on the couch.

Everything points to Jake being MoonFire. Calling me TraumaBull. His voice. It's deep, yet soft. Submissive, yet strong. Like he knows what he wants and isn't afraid to beg for it.

And fuck me, how sexy he sounds when he's pleading.

I don't know how long I'm daydreaming about MoonFire and Adam, but when my phone vibrates in my pocket, I nearly come. I had no idea my hard on had taken on a life of its own. My tip was against my phone. The vibration nearly sent me straight to hell.

I sit up quickly as I answer. "Yeah," I say into the phone. The phone number isn't known to me, but it's local. I'm hoping it's Jake.

"Hey, it's Jake. Someone came in and dropped some stuff off for Raina. I didn't get names. I should've, but he asked for me, so I assume this is who you were talking about."

"Yeah. Yeah, it was. I'll be right in. Thank you for doing this for me."

"You should know, he looked really upset. And also, since he left there's been a black undercover squad sitting outside."

"Fuck me," I grumble.

"I can meet you somewhere else. Make sure I'm not tailed. I parked out back. I can leave the back way and take backroads."

I nod. "Can you meet me at Kaasa's?"

"Absolutely. If I'm tailed, I'll call you back."

"Thanks, man. I'm sorry for dragging you into this."

"Hey. Don't be. I'm happy to help out. I'll see you soon. I'm just getting off work right now."

"Okay. I'll meet you there."

We both hang up. I make my way up to Raina's room and knock on the door.

"Yeah?" she says in her quiet voice.

"I'm just going to get your stuff, Raina. Pick what you want for dinner. I'll make it when I'm home. And you know the rule. Don't go outside or leave the house. I know it's frustrating, but Adam is close. We just need to give him time."

"I understand, Uncle."

I'm really glad she listens well and understands what Adam is trying to do. A lot of teenage girls would be hell to deal with right now, but not her. She's always been a dream of a niece. Even though she got scared and ran, I trust that we're past that.

❄❄❄

I park my bike behind Kaasa's and lean against the side of the building so I can see who comes in and out of the lot.

I watch as a really beat up Kia drives into the lot. Jake texted and said that was his car. I don't see anyone following him, definitely not an undercover squad, but I wait until he parks and gets out before I approach.

It gives me more time to see if anyone pulls in. He ducks back in his car and grabs a backpack out. When he stands back up, he throws it over his shoulder and looks around.

I don't see anyone at all turn into the parking lot, so I get his attention and wave him over. He simply nods before walking inside. I raise an eyebrow, but just as I'm about to follow, I see a black car pull into the lot. It doesn't look undercover, but who the fuck knows what those assholes drive to try and trick people.

"Son of a bitch," I murmur. The car parks at the far end of the lot. No one gets out. "What the fuck is going on?" This is way too much for a sixteen-year-old runaway.

Adam was released from custody within twenty minutes of being arrested. The video was quickly proven fake. So, why the hell are they going through so much trouble when they've already decided that Raina ran away? Per Caden fucking Andrews himself.

I hear a low whistle behind me and glance over my shoulder. Jake is at the back of the building. He's fucking smart, and I love it. I take one more glance at the car before turning and heading towards Jake.

When I reach him, he's removing a pink backpack from the black one he was carrying. He looks up at me. "He brought in her pink backpack with all of her homework and everything for the next two weeks. I have a backpack I take to work with me with a book and change of clothes just in case I don't want to go right home after work. I shoved hers into mine."

"Good thing you did because you were followed."

"I know." He stands, concern etched on his sexy, chiseled features. "The thing is, I don't think that guy has to do with whatever this is."

I raise an eyebrow as I take the backpack he gives me. "What do you mean?" I sling the backpack over my shoulders as I wait for him to answer.

He looks down and shakes his head. "It's nothing. Really. I'm probably being paranoid."

"Jake," my voice drops, and I have to control my breathing when his eyes snap submissively to mine. "Tell me what's going on."

He sighs and looks down. "It's just that I think… for the past couple of days… someone has been watching me. But it's never the same vehicle I see following me. It's never the same number that calls and hangs up."

My protective instincts are instantaneously in overdrive. *Someone is stalking him? Not on my fucking watch.* He doesn't look scared, but I know he doesn't feel safe either.

I put a hand on his shoulder, hoping to comfort him. "You have my number." I smile reassuringly when he looks up at me, a hopeful glint in his pretty eyes. I squeeze his shoulder. "Call me if you get uncomfortable." I don't use the word 'scared' because any guy I know would scoff at that and hide behind their pride of being tough and not afraid of anything. "I mean it. Just call."

He nods, a small smile on his face. "Okay."

"How about I follow you out of here? I can keep an eye on that car. If he follows, I'll take care of it." I wink with a grin.

As I'd hoped, Jake laughs. "What are you going to do? Run him off the road?"

My grin widens and becomes more mischievous. "If that's what I need to do."

He laughs again. "Okay. Should we get a move on? I have a pizza waiting to be picked up."

"That sounds amazing. Makes me want delivery. Let's go so I can take care of this problem." I grin like I'm teasing, but there's nothing humorous about what I'm about to do.

I put my helmet on and follow Jake around the building like we weren't trying to hide or anything. My eyes fall on the black car. The closer I look at it, the easier it is to see that it's not an unmarked squad. It's too beat up, but it's the rims that give it away. Cops run with Run Flat tires with rims that always look new. They have to. If they get into a chase, the tires are the most important part. Running with rusty rims, like this car has, poses a huge threat. Never know what's going to happen with them.

"Wait for me," I tell him. "I parked my bike in the back. When you see me pull around, you can go. I'll follow the car."

"Got it."

I love how well he listens. I jog around the corner and to the back of the diner to grab my bike. I start it and drive it around to the front. I stop and wait as Jake backs out of his spot and leaves. It doesn't take the car long to follow, but I see he's looking at me like he's gauging what I'm about to do.

He can't see who I am with my helmet on, and I love that it gives me anonymity. I don't have a front plate. My rear one is flipped up. There's no way he can identify me. We have an entire biker group full of sportsbike riders. Lots of people in the area ride white bikes. I doubt very seriously he'll know I'm on an R7.

Once he makes the decision to leave the parking lot, I wait for him to turn the direction Jake went.

MoonFire.

The more I think about his voice on the phone, the more I'm convinced I'm right. I told him when I was fucking around with him on Discord that a dom always knows certain things about his sub. I wasn't kidding. I knew he was touching himself. It was like I could sense it. I wanted him to touch himself with me.

In this case, I just feel it in my heart, my stomach, my fucking cock. I know Jake is MoonFire. He's mine.

I know he's also Adam's. I know they've had a couple of nights together. We've talked about them. We've talked about my night with him, too. There was no jealousy between us. We're fine with sharing. The issue is that I don't know if Adam knows who MoonFire is in real life. And if he does, I don't know how this relationship is going to go. It's one thing fucking around together with someone behind a screen. It's quite another to have that person right here.

And not only that, how would he feel being with me, too? Would that option even be on the table? Or would we just be focused solely on Jake?

So many questions run though my mind, but they are immediately silenced when Black Car Asshole makes a move. He speeds up. He's way too close to Jake. From behind, I can see very clearly what he's trying to do, and I'm not allowing it. I crouch and hit the throttle, speeding up myself. I catch up to him in no time.

Before he has a chance to react, I'm next to his window and swerving towards him. He's wearing all black clothes and a mask. He's definitely seen one too many bags of chips.

His head snaps towards me. I can see his wide eyes through the simple ski mask as he veers away from me.

But he's not paying attention to what's next to him. It's not steep, but he careens into the ditch and right up the side of the road. He crashes into a tree. I see Jake pull over out of the corner of my eye as I, myself, stop. Jake starts getting out.

"Go!" I command, waving him on. He nods and gets back in his car. As he drives away, the guy opens his door.

"Motherfucker! Watch where you're going! What the fuck is wrong with you?"

I chuckle before revving it and taking off, leaving him and his wrecked car. He didn't have injuries from what I could see. I don't think his airbag even went off. Typical, considering the wreck that car was before it crashed.

As I head for home, I decide immediately that I need to call Adam to see if he agrees with me about Jake being MoonFire. If the pieces I've put together make sense.

And if he thinks I'm on the right track, then we have a lot to talk about…

Chapter Six

❄ Adam ❄

"What's up, Adrian? How's my little girl?" I ask when I answer my phone.

"She's good. You can talk to her in a minute, but listen. MoonFire. We need to talk about him."

I raise an eyebrow at the urgency in his voice. "Okay? I already told you, though. I'm good sharing with you."

"That's one thing we need to discuss. Can you sit down? I can hear you pacing."

I stop pacing, not even realizing I was doing it. But to be honest, it's been all I've been doing for the past few days. Ever since I found my runaway daughter. To ease his mind, though, I sit down in my recliner. Whatever he has to tell me about MoonFire sounds important.

"Okay. Sitting down."

"It's Jake. From Cozy Bean."

"What?" I raise a confused eyebrow as I lean back in the chair and put up the footrest. It actually feels good to sit down.

"It's Jake. I'm sure."

"Slow down. What are you talking about? How do you know?"

He takes a deep breath and lets it out. I can hear him sitting down on his leather couch. "Raina wanted to keep up with school. I don't blame her. So, we found a way to get her the work she needs. We had her boyfriend drop it at the Cozy Bean. Jake met me at Kaasa's. When I called Cozy Bean to see if he was there to help out with this, he called me TraumaBull."

I furrow my brows, the lines in my face crinkling even deeper. "I feel like you missed a big chunk of this explanation."

"When I was talking to him asking him for the favor. He answered the phone when I called. I said his name. Told him it was me. Asked him for a favor. There was a bit of a pause before he called me TraumaBull. Low. He was questioning it. Didn't say it loud."

"And what did you say?"

"I was shocked. I just said 'what' before he recovered."

"It sounds like he knows you're TraumaBull. How do you know he's MoonFire?"

"Same way he knows. His voice. I sat there and pretty much obsessed over it. It's absolutely him. He said one day on Discord he worked in a coffee shop. He said he was going to get a friend from work to join our guild. There's a girl there he's always working with. I've heard them talk about gaming a few times. It's all too coincidental."

"I don't believe in coincidence."

"My point. Neither do I. But this? Way, way too coincidental to be a coincidence in any manner."

It's my turn to pause. Thinking about it, Jake really does sound a lot like MoonFire. Everyone sounds different when over a headset as opposed to in person, but not so different that voices can never be recognized.

He also spends a lot of time watching us and flirting. It makes me think he's suspicious about if we're WOW players or not. Like he has an idea but is trying to put all the pieces together. It's possible Adrian being on the phone triggered something for Jake that made all of the pieces fit all of the sudden.

I pinch the bridge of my nose with a chuckle. "It does make sense."

"Yeah. Way too much sense. Which means we have a lot of shit to talk about, Adam. Serious shit."

Shit I absolutely don't want to talk about in the slightest. "Can we deal with this after I get Raina? My attorney -"

Adrian cuts me off. "No. We can't. We've been running around this for years. I know I have. And sitting here thinking about all of this stuff… Man, I know you have feelings for me. I know you have for a long time. And I'm right there. I was just too much of a fucking coward to say it."

I nearly choke. Leave it to Adrian to cut right to the chase. He's never been one to beat around the bush. Well, I guess on everything else but me.

Maybe that's why we get along so well. I feel the same way about things as he does.

I guess I even feel the same about him as he does me. I never thought I'd see the day we'd be here.

"There's no easy way to say it, Adam," Adrian says a little less forcefully and with a lot quieter of a voice. Softer tone. "I've been fucking head over heels for years. I feel like an idiot because I held back. Had I paid attention, I'd have seen you felt the same. You've never been that great at hiding things. At least from me. Maybe from the rest of the world, but not me. I was just too wrapped up in my own feelings to see it."

I sigh and lean my head back, reclining even more. "I do have feelings for you. Strong ones. I never said anything because I didn't think you felt the same, and I didn't want to say it and ruin the friendship. That's what has always been the most important thing to me. And it still is, Adrian."

"The friendship won't be ruined. It's the foundation of everything. It's what we're built on."

I shake my head. "Every friend who starts a relationship with another friend says the same thing. And what happens? Something goes wrong. Everything changes. They break up. Never speak again. The friendship is ruined. The relationship is gone. Both are broken shells of themselves with no one to lean on because the only person they had is gone. I don't want that."

Adrian sighs. "I know. I get it. I do. But -"

It's my turn to cut him off. "No. I can't do it. I can't risk losing you. We can share Jake. Hell, I'll stay away from him if that's what you want, but you and I? We can't happen. We can't. I need you in my life. I don't want to risk something blowing up and losing you." I don't say it, but I wouldn't survive it.

"Adam -"

"Adrian. Please. This is something I'm standing firm on."

There's a long pause, and if I didn't hear his breathing on the other end, I'd think he hung up. Finally, he sighs. "So, where do we go from here, Adam? Knowing we have feelings for each other. How do we just keep being friends with that kind of knowledge in our minds and hearts?"

"We ignore this conversation happened. Except for the part about MoonFire being Jake. You tell me if you want to share him or want him to yourself. We keep our relationship. That's what we do."

"And what if Jake wants us both? Together? What then? What if your fear is keeping us from making the best decision of our lives? Think about that."

Without another word, Adrian hangs up on me. In all of the years I've known him, my entire life, he's never hung on me. We've never left a conversation like this.

What if I really am making a piss poor decision based on fear? What if a relationship with him is what we've both been waiting for our entire lives?

But what if I'm right? What if a relationship beyond what we have now is what breaks us?

Or what if I just buried our relationship simply by having this conversation?

❄❄❄

"Guys, I don't know how else to say this," I begin, rubbing my head. "But we used to be a good guild. Now we have six people, our Officers and Team Leads, no less, who are literally carrying the entire guild on our backs. I'm kicking everyone tonight. I'll happily start the fuck over."

"Just give it a bit, BloodKnight. Everyone took this loss hard," TraumaBull says in an effort to calm me down. It works. It always works. "Let's take the week to practice. We have our next raid on Saturday. It gives everyone time to figure things out. There are a couple new people. So, let's just take the time to become a cohesive unit. Talk to each other. Get to know our newbies."

I let out a long sigh. My eyes are closed. I don't intend on opening them. I'm done with today. "We need a lot of improvement, guys. We lost against easy bosses."

"We know, BloodKnight." MoonFire's melodic voice cuts through all the bullshit running through my head. And like TraumaBull, he calms the fire in my veins. "Everyone feels bad about it. One thing went wrong, then many others. I even messed up a couple of times because I wasn't paying attention to the right thing."

I nod. "Yeah, we all messed up. I didn't call to taunt off. I missed a cool down and made you scramble."

"I kept getting caught in the fucking trap and fucking freezing," another player grumbles. "I couldn't get out of it because I was so slowed down. Every time I recovered, I got it again."

"I couldn't heal fast enough," Librii, our new Healer, adds. "I'd throw group heals, and then I'd have to heal TraumaBull. Which was totally fine, but while I was healing him, the group would need a heal again. I couldn't keep up."

Lachlan growls. "I couldn't keep up with them either because I was taking adds. This was an impossible run."

"It was," I agree, "but it shouldn't have been."

"Definitely not," one of our younger members says. He's one of our best Hunters. "But like was already said, I kept getting caught in the Boss's Circle of Doom. I couldn't get out of it. When I did, I was slowed down again. I couldn't control adds at all. I couldn't even control myself."

"It's okay," I say. "We'll go ahead and run some dungeons through the week. Next raid will be a lot better."

"That's the spirit, fearless leader!" another guild member says. I grin, feeling a lot more like myself.

Though, I'm still pretty pissed. I've been irrationally angry ever since the conversation with Adrian earlier. I'm irritated he hung up on me. I might have deserved it, but he's never done that before.

"Alright, guys. It's late. I know some of you work early in the morning. Head on out. Thanks for everything tonight." My comment about working early is meant for Jake. I use a dominant tone so he knows who I'm talking about. I wait as everyone drops off, Jake being the first. When it's just me and Adrian, I sigh. "You've had me fucked up all damn day."

"Good. You need to think about things. And not take it out on everyone else. You had everyone in a fucking tizzy because you were off your game."

Leave it to fucking Adrian Sloan to call my ass out in such a direct manner. I hate it. My dominant feathers are standing straight up. The growl that leaves my throat and escapes through my lips isn't something I can stop even if I wanted to.

Which I don't.

I want Adrian to know he's playing a dangerous game here. One where there can be no winners. Only heartbreak and devastation.

"If I were there right now, Adrian, I'd have you over my knee. You're so fucking frustrating sometimes."

He gives me a long pause before finally gracing me with his voice. "Are we talking about me calling you out in the game? Or are you still salty about earlier?"

"Both," I growl. I'm irritated because I know he's right. About the game at least. If I'm being honest with myself, I know he's right about everything else, too. But my fears are far too deep-rooted to listen.

"Listen, man. You can be pissed off at me all you want. I can take it. I've seen you at your best and worst. But I'm not sitting around letting you bark at everyone else just to take out the aggressions and stress you got going on towards me and life. You know you were being an asshole in that raid tonight. Everyone lost morale."

Again, I know he's right. I rub my head because I'm not willing to give up the fight. "I'd spank your ass red."

"Yeah? That's what you want to do to me?"

"If I was there? Yeah. Because I'm that fucking frustrated."

"Would my pants be down?" His tone has dropped to sexy and flirty.

It pisses me off even more.

But two can play this game. If he really wants to go down this path, well, he'll see how it would really be if I allowed it to happen.

Which I fucking won't.

"Yeah. They would be. Underwear and all. You'd be bare ass, dick dangling down my thigh." That came out a lot more raspy than I intended it to, so I clear my throat. My hand inadvertently grips my cock.

"I'd be dripping precome on your leg anticipating what happens next." His octave drops even lower, and I hate it.

But I really don't.

I love that his tone is all for me.

"I'd spank it for every dick twitch I feel; every single time my own cock jumps." I let my eyes fall closed. There's no harm in indulging in the fantasy. I'll never let it happen in real life. "And once it's good and red for me," I stroke my dick slowly, not letting myself take it out of my sweats yet, "I'd rub it, gently, only to do it all fucking over again."

"I'd move myself down a little so my head is in your lap. I'd be driving you crazy rubbing my nose slowly up and down your dick, making you hard for me. I'd inhale your scent, memorizing it, while my ass is in the air for you."

My fingers squeeze my throbbing length as I let out a low moan. "Would you suck it?"

"While you stroke my cock until I make a mess of your hand. I'd swallow everything you gave me until your balls were empty."

I can hear him stroking his own to dick to the thoughts of that, and I can't help but pull my own out. I give myself long, hard, and fast caresses until I'm so close to blowing my load that I can't hold it back anymore. Cum flies from my shaft and hits my desk, chin, and arms while it gushes down my hand onto my balls.

Adrian's satiated moans tell me he just released, and all I can think about in the afterglow is how good he'd look covered in my cum.

A few minutes later, after we both come down, I find myself right back in my head. "This was a stupid thing to do Adrian," I say, my voice way more shaky than I'd like it. "This can't happen between us."

He chuckles. "It didn't happen between us. It happened between BloodKnight and TraumaBull."

I open my mouth to retort, but I can't. There's nothing to say to that. I know I won't win the argument. I'm far too tired; too spent.

And too fucking unbalanced…

Chapter Seven

(One Week Later)

I wipe my face with my shirt before taking it off completely and tossing it on the railing near Henry's door. I'm more irritated at myself than I am the lawn or the weather. I can't focus on anything but TraumaBull and BloodKnight.

Sloan and Damien.

No one has confirmed it yet, but I know that TraumaBull is Sloane and BloodKnight is Damien. There's no other explanation. They both sound exactly like their characters. They act like their characters. They give me the same chills as they do in the game when I hear them.

I've been with both of them several times over the past week, and it convinces me even more.

I've also seen them in the coffee shop a lot. I've texted Sloane a few times just to see if he'd answer if I asked how he's doing or what's going on. He answered every time I texted. He's even told me several times that I made his day just by texting.

So, why am I so pissed off? Because I know who they are. I want to tell them who I am, but I don't know how they'll take it. I've dropped several hints, practically given it all away. Neither of them have said a word.

And that makes me feel like they are completely disinterested in me outside of the game or a virtual relationship. Sloan didn't want to see me in person outside the coffee shop when I texted him about lunch a couple of days ago.

I groan out loud as I finish the weed wacking. I need to get my mind off them, and get back to my life. I'm getting more and more irritable with the lack of sleep I'm getting. I get up early for work, then hurry home so I can get online to see if they're on so I can't talk to them. I haven't been over to Henry's in a few days. That's not like me. I try to get over and see him every day just to make sure he's doing alright.

I shut the weed wacker off and prop it against the stairs. The Texas heat makes me want to down a gallon of water, but I ran out of that halfway through mowing.

Like a godsend, Henry pops out with a glass that looks like an icy invitation. He holds it out to me. "Thought you could use this," he says, his tired voice betraying the bright smile on his face. "Thanks for grabbing me those few things from the store today."

I take the lemonade gratefully and nod. "You're very welcome. Always here if you need anything." I close my eyes after putting the glass to my lips. I gulp down the sweet and tangy liquid like it's the last thing I'll ever put in my mouth and down my throat.

The thought that brings to my head makes me swallow wrong. I start coughing.

"Oh my," Henry says, alarmed. "Are you okay?"

I nod as I pound on my chest like an ape. "Yep!" My pitch is unnaturally high, but there's no way I'm breathing a word about how I just pictured two men's dicks in my mouth fucking it like they're insatiable and will never get enough. "Just down the wrong hatch!"

"Well, be more careful, boy. You're liable to give me a heart attack." He grins, and I laugh. One of my favorite things about Henry is his sense of humor. He's been sick, but he can still joke proudly about it.

"I wouldn't want that." I finish off the glass and give it back to him with a smile. "Now that's some good lemonade."

He nods happily. "I'm telling you. Country Time does it right."

"That they do." I glance at my watch. It's nearly eight at night, and I still haven't eaten. I made sure Henry did, though. I bought him a rotisserie chicken at the store while I was there. I got it all cut up for him before I went out to mow his lawn. "I suppose I should get going. Probably grab something to eat."

"Got some chicken left over. Would you like that?"

"No, sir." I laugh. "It sounds good, though. I'm gonna run by the store and grab myself some. I want you to eat. I'll come by tomorrow and have lunch with you. We'll play cards."

Henry's face lights up. "Okay!"

I give him a hug and send him inside. It's too hot out here for him. I grab my sweaty shirt and groan when I put it back on. It's soaked. I grit my teeth and ignore it as I pick up the weed wacker. I walk it to the garage and put it away before closing the garage door. I climb in my car and look up to the window I know Henry is standing by. He always sees me off. He tries to look happy, but I can see a little pain behind his smile. I'm sure he's getting lonely the older he gets.

As I'm backing out of the driveway, I notice a beat up white vehicle with blacked out windows pulls out of a parking spot behind me. I'm immediately on edge. I haven't had anyone follow me since the night I met Sloan at Kaasa's. I guess I was naive enough to believe this shit was over.

"I'm not going to freak out," I mumble to myself.

My eyes are glued to my rearview mirror. I make several random turns, and the white car follows my every move. Not wanting to go to my apartment, I make my way to the store. I know there are cameras in the parking lot. Once I park, I have no intention of getting out of my car, but at least the cameras can be my witness if anything happens while I wait for my Wogen to show up.

"Hey, Jake. What's up? You okay? I thought you'd be online," Adrian says, his deep, velvety voice laced with concern.

"I was with Henry. He's an older guy I help out. He lives a couple blocks away from my apartment building."

"Ah. Yeah, that makes sense. I think you mentioned him before. You gonna jump on soon? Me and Damien are on. We thought we could run some daily stuff."

"Uh. Yeah. Maybe."

"Maybe?"

I watch the white car park a few spots up from me. He's in the row behind me so in order for me to see him, I have to watch my side mirror or strain my head. "Sloan, uh… I'm being followed again. I'm at Marketplace. It's a white car. Blacked out windows. Before, with the other car, I could see someone inside. They were wearing a mask. This time, I can't see anything. The windows are too dark."

"I can't leave my house, but I'm sending Damien. He's on his way right now. Sit tight. Don't hang up with me until you see him. Do you remember what his bike looks like?"

"Yeah. All black. It says something that starts with a 'K' on the side."

"Kawasaki. He'll be there in five. Don't get out of your car. Where's the other car parked?"

"The row behind me, but he's a few spots up. I can see him in my side mirror."

"Tell me if he does anything. I have Damien on another phone. I can tell him what's going on."

"Okay." My heart is racing. I don't know if it's out of fear, or the fact that Damien is coming.

It's both. I know damn well it's both.

A few moments later, I see the door of the car open. I stare silently and wide eyed as someone gets out. He's wearing a mask. He's fairly tall. Muscular. I know it's the same person. He has the same build. Same mask.

"Fuck," I whisper as I make sure all of my doors are locked. "Fuck, fuck, fuck!" That racing heartbeat turns to unadulterated panic.

"What's happening?"

"He's out of his car! And he's walking towards me!" I reach down and turn the key in the intuition. The car doesn't start. "No!" I shout. "My car isn't starting!" I frantically keep turning the key, but nothing happens.

"He's a block away, Jake! Hang tight! Keep trying to start your car!"

I glance over and see that he's carrying a tire iron. Before I can say anything to Sloan about it, the guy swings the tire iron into my back window.

"Fuck!" I scream as I duck.

Another swing. This time into the window just behind mine.

"He's got a tire iron, Sloan! He's swinging it into my windows!"

Another shattering blow directly to my driver's side window has me letting out another scream.

"He's almost there, Jake!" Sloan shouts.

Blow after blow.

My window finally shatters.

I try climbing over my center console to get to the other side. I need to get out of here. Run.

But it's too late. My door swings open, and I feel hands on me. I fight. I swing my hand back. My phone lands against the side of his head and flies out of my hand, but it doesn't seem to matter. It doesn't faze him in the slightest.

So, I kick. I don't bother aiming. I just need the blows to land somewhere. Any damage I can cause is good for me. It gives me time.

I need time.

All the time I can get.

"Get the fuck off me!" I yell as I kick.

But my kicks don't do anything either. I know I'm landing them, but the guy is a fucking machine. He's like a terminator. Unbreakable. Unable to be hurt. He laughs the harder I fight until he finally gets sick of my antics and grabs my legs.

"Stop fucking around," he growls as he yanks me out of the car.

Hard.

So hard that I fly out of it. My head hits the edge of my car before it lands hard on the cement parking lot. I instantly start seeing black dots floating in front of my face, but I know passing out would be the absolute end of me. I won't survive it.

I have to hold on a little longer. I don't know where my phone is, but it has to be near because Sloan is yelling something about Damien. I can't quite understand all of the words, but I know he's close. He has to be.

Unwilling to give up, I twist my body and start clawing at the ground beneath me. If I can get under my car, I can get away. I kick and twist until I feel my legs fall to the ground. Without wasting a second, I start crawling under my car, but it's too low to the ground. I can't fit.

"Fuck!" I scream.

It doesn't take long before the guy is on me again. He's wrenching me off the ground with an arm around my throat. I try to drop my body to throw him off center, but he only moves with me and tightens his grip.

I'm going to pass out. Between the two shots to my head and the lack of oxygen from the chokehold, I'm not going to make it. No matter how hard I fight, my movements are getting weaker and slowing down. My vision is getting darker.

And then I hear it.

The rumbling sound of a bike screaming through the lot.

"Get off him!"

BloodKnight. That's him. That's his voice. It's powerful. Unmistakable.

I feel a hard shove from behind and succumb to gravity, landing hard on the ground once more. I'm too weak to even attempt to get up, so I don't. I cough and sputter with my cheek against the ground. I'm dizzy as fuck, and I'm fighting the darkness with everything I am.

I don't know what's going on above me, but there's yelling. It sounds muffled and far away. My eyes start closing.

"No…" I groan. "No… fuck… please…"

"Hey, stay with me. I got you," Damien says. He looks blurry. Fading on the edges. "Jake, come on. Don't close your fucking eyes."

I flutter them, but it's no use. I feel them closing, and no matter how much I want to listen to my heroic Night Elf, it's no use.

"I'm sorry," I whisper as everything goes midnight black…

❄❄❄

"Mmm…" I groan as I blink awake. I rub my eyes and yawn.

Then wince and hiss at the pain.

"Don't move too much."

It's *his* voice.

Damien.

BloodKnight.

Wait.

I blink a few more times. The room is dark. Too dark for it to be my room. My room is never this black, even at midnight.

The bed. It's way too soft. My sheets are cotton. The sheets under me are way too soft against my skin to be cotton.

Skin? Shouldn't I be wearing clothes? Am I wearing anything? What the fuck is happening?

"Where am I?" I murmur.

"What do you remember?"

I blink a few more times trying to orient myself and ignore the pain in my fucking head. It feels like a drill straight through my brain.

"Fuck. I don't know."

"Try."

I sigh and instantly regret it. "Why does my head hurt so much?" The bed dips beside me. I see Damien, though barely.

"I need you to be a good boy, Jake. I need you to try remembering for me." The dominant edge of his voice is there, but there's something else. Something I can't quite decipher.

Needing to obey him, I close my eyes and try. It takes me time, I don't know how much, but bits and pieces start to come back. "I called Sloan. I was being followed."

"Yes," Damien chokes out.

Concern.

Fear.

That's what I heard before. He's scared.

But why?

Not understanding the reason I feel I need to reach out for his hand, I give in. The moment my skin meets his, proverbial sparks fly. It's like a full electric shock is coursing through my body, leaving nothing but ruin in its wake. But it's not until his hand squeezes mine like he's making sure I'm really real that I realize there's no turning back. I need him as much as he obviously needs me.

His touch, the protective vibes I feel radiating off him, makes me feel safe. And that feeling allows everything to rush back to me. It crashes over me like a tidal wave, threatening to pull me under. I gasp for air as my eyes fly open.

"Hey. Breathe… I'm right here. You're safe." Damien's voice exudes exactly what he promises. His thumb rubs over the back of my hand. My heart slows before I even register its beating too fast.

I take a deep breath and allow my eyes to fall closed again. "He got to the car. Destroyed it. Pulled me out. My head hit my car and the ground. You got there just in time. I passed out." I slowly open my eyes as he squeezes my hand. "But I woke up in the hospital."

"I got you there. They checked you out. The police are dealing with your car. The guy got away, but I got a plate."

I nod, but only slightly. Too much movement will make that pain start again. I don't want any part of it. "Thank you. For… uh… coming. I'm sorry it's happening. I'm no one, so I don't know why this person is after me."

"First of all, there's always a reason. We just have to figure it out. Second, don't ever, ever, ever, fucking say you're no one. Ever. If you weren't laid out in my bed right now hurt, you'd be over my knee."

I can't stop the gasp that leaves my lips. "I… didn't… mean that I wasn't someone. Just that -"

"Stop. Stop. There's no way you can finish that sentence without it being an insult to yourself. And I'm not fucking tolerating that bullshit, Jake. I'm not going to forget you said it. The first chance I get, you'll be over my knee regretting every word."

I open my mouth to say something, but no words come out.

Because Damien's mouth crashes down on mine.

It's not just a regular kiss. It's an all consuming kiss that makes every nerve tingle, every blood cell boil, and my brain stop functioning. I don't remember how to breathe. My heart either stops beating or beats so fast that I can't feel it. I'm sure gravity ceases to exist, and I'm going to be flung into outer space.

Oh fuck.

Fuck me.

Is this really happening?

Are all of my dreams coming true?

After the shock subsides, I gain enough sense to start kissing him back, but before I can, he's pulling away.

"Holy hell. I shouldn't have done that. I'm so fucking sorry, Jake."

"What?"

“I’m sorry.”

I reach up and caress my lower lip with my thumb. I watch in bewilderment as he flees the room. Seconds later, the door closes behind him, and he’s gone.

I’m left with so many unanswered questions, but mostly…

…what did I do to make him run?

Chapter Eight

❄ Adrian ❄

I sigh at the knock on the door and get up. I've been watching a movie with Raina. Something she wanted. I don't know what it's called, but she deserves a day free of stress. So, I made snacks and let her pick the movie. I'm not sure if I regret it or if I enjoy whatever romcom she picked.

That's a question for another day. Not something I want to explore today. Why does Ryan Reynolds have to be so hot? Fuck him and this movie.

I move the shade covering the floor to ceiling window near my door and shake my head with a low growl.

"Psst!" I wave to get Raina's attention. She looks over at me with wide eyes. I point upstairs. She nods and grabs her blanket, scurrying for the stairs. This shit needs to be over. That girl can't just sit in hiding forever.

I open the door and don't say a word to the asshole Lieutenant standing on the other side of it. I fold my arms over my chest and block his entrance into the house.

"I know she's here, Adrian," Caden says to me. He looks worn out.

"Got a warrant?"

He holds his hands in front of him in surrender. "No. I'm not asking to come in. I'm not even going to ask you to bring her down. I know she's safe. That's all that matters."

I narrow my eyes suspiciously. "What the fuck is wrong with you?"

His hands drop to his sides, and he shakes his head as he looks down. It takes him a few seconds to look up at me again. "There was video footage of Raina getting on the back of Adam's bike the night she disappeared. We've been able to get warrants to search both his and your places because of that video and other bits and pieces of evidence we've collected over the past week."

"Look, Caden. I'm not -"

"No. Stop. Please. Let me finish, man."

I glare at him, but give him a nod.

"The video was faked. It was given to our tech team. A lot of other shit was disproven by our forensics team. I found a cover up within the department. I'm working to take it down. I talked to Adam's attorney, but the DA is still going forward with this shit, even though he has no evidence. Notes were missing from my desk this morning. I keep my door locked. I looked to see who entered my office, and the cameras had a convenient glitch at that time. I don't believe in coincidence. I'm here because there's another team calling for a warrant right now. And I'm positive they used my notes. I had my brother stake out your house and took notes from a call with him last night. They have an arrest warrant for you."

I raise an eyebrow, alarmed. "The fuck did you have in those notes?"

"A lot of shit that can be used against us both, man. I need you to trust me right now. Take my truck." He hands me the keys. "Get Raina. Go to my house and get my wife. And then get the fuck out of here. I'll take your bike. They'll pull me over thinking I'm you. I'll let them. I need your plate removed on your bike so I can say it's mine."

Way too many thoughts are racing through my head. I look past him trying to see any sign of anyone else about to storm my house the second I take his keys. I may not like Caden, but I know him. He takes his job seriously. If he's breaking rules and protocol, I know he has more reasons than I have for not caring for him in the slightest.

I reach for the keys and take them as I look over my shoulder, then back at him. "I swear, Caden. If you're trying to jack us up, I'll come for you."

"I'm not. I know there's no love lost with us, but we grew up together. You, me, Adam, and Brax. My brothers. I know some fucked up shit happened, but I'm not fucking around right now. This is my job. Your life and the life of a child depend on me being really fucking good at it."

I nod and step aside so he can walk in. He does, quickly and with purpose. "We don't have a lot of time, Sloan."

"Raina!" I call as I start cleaning up the snacks. "I need you to grab your stuff! Fast!"

"Yes, sir!" she calls from the top of the stairs.

To my surprise, Caden helps me clean up. It takes only a couple of minutes. I rush up the stairs to grab a bag for myself. Raina runs out of her room just as I'm passing. We barely avoid a collision.

"Got everything?"

She nods. "Yeah."

"Go downstairs. Caden is down there. Lieutenant Andrews. I know he's been the one here serving the warrants and shit, but things changed. Trust him."

"Do you?"

"Yeah. I do." It's the truth. I do trust him. Might not like him, but I know I can trust him.

"Okay." She hurries down the stairs.

I put his keys in my pocket and grab a duffel bag. I throw what I need for a few days into it.

"Aiden! Time to move!" Caden calls. "They got the warrant! On their way!"

"Coming!" I jog out of my room and down the stairs. Caden is standing by the door with Raina.

"Keys to your bike," he commands, hand held out.

I take them off the hook. "That has my house key on it. Guard it with your fucking life."

"Plates?"

"It's not on the bike. I run with it in my backpack because every cop in this area loves to fuck up biker's lives." I smirk because he can't deny it.

He returns the smirk. "Gives us something to do on a boring night. Go. Get out of here. GPS is set to take you to my house. My wife knows you're coming. She'll guide you to our cabin."

"You gonna tell me why I need to grab her? Do I need to prepare for a fight?"

"Precaution. If I'm going up against other cops, I want her out of here. Protect her. Please."

I nod and shake his hand as I hurry Raina out the door. We jog to the truck and throw our stuff in.

"What's going on?" Raina asks me as I pull out of my driveway.

"I don't fully know, princess."

"Is my dad in danger?"

I don't know how to answer that, so I answer honestly. "I don't know. But I trust Caden. I do."

We both fall silent as I follow the GPS out of town towards Caden's home. I watch to make sure we aren't being followed.

"I'm scared, Uncle Aiden," Raina says quietly, staring down at her shoes.

"I know, princess. But I'm not letting anything happen to you."

"What about Bentley? He said he was being followed by the police now."

I take a deep breath. "I wish I had answers for you, Raina."

We fall silent once more as I turn into Caden's house. Krissy, Caden's wife, is sitting with two suitcases and their dog on the porch. When she sees Caden's truck, she immediately gets up. I park and get out. Raina quietly moves to the backseat without me giving the order.

"Hey, Aiden," Krissy says as I grab her bags. "Long time no see." The last time she saw me was last year at the Ice Sculpting contest held each year during the Piper Falls Christmas Fest.

The Piper Falls Sportsbike Club puts it on. We all get together to host it, but we all also chip in for a ten-thousand dollar scholarship. We get area businesses to help us out with several five-hundred dollar gift cards for each participant. We hold the event at Papi's Bar and Grill. Papi's chips in a one-hundred dollar gift card to any teen that shows up to watch that isn't involved in the contest. The entire thing is put on for kids between the ages of thirteen and seventeen because this is the age group that is forgotten about the most during the holiday season.

It's my favorite event of the entire fest. Everyone comes together and puts aside differences during the season just so we can make it great for everyone else.

"Yeah," I tell her. I put her bags in the backseat after the dog gets in and settles right into Raina. "You okay back here?" I ask her. She nods but says nothing, just drops her hand to the dog's head.

Krissy gets into the front seat and grabs Caden's phone. "He said he'll be at the cabin before the sun goes down. He wants to get Adam."

My heart both skips a beat and starts racing.

Adam.

"My dad will be there?" Raina asks hopefully.

Krissy smiles reassuringly, but I can see the worry in her eyes as I climb back in the driver's side. "He will be."

For the first time in days, Raina smiles. Not the fake one she puts on when she's trying to convince me she's doing okay. A real, genuine smile.

Krissy puts the phone back in the holder, and I glance at it as I turn the truck around. "Just follow that?" I ask.

"Yes. It's about an hour away."

"Okay." I drive to the highway and make a left, heading even further out of town.

The entire time I'm driving, I can't help but think about Adam and Jake. Caden made it seem like this whole fucking thing is about to explode. Secrets, conspiracies, and vicious lies seem to be the name of whatever game we're playing.

I know Adam can handle himself, but I worry about him regardless. I'm in love with him, yeah, but above that, he's my best friend. I'd never want to see anything happen to him. It would kill me.

But Jake… He's got this stalker now. Being all the way out in the fucking woods at a cabin protecting Raina, myself, and Krissy from other cops is crazy. But not being able to be there for him is another feeling entirely. I need to be there but can't. I don't like that. Panic takes over, but I manage to calm down.

And then it happens all over again.

He's defenseless out there against a psychopath.

I'm so lost in my head, I completely miss the turn. I only come out of it when Krissy nudges my arm.

"Aiden?" She nudges my arm again.

"Yeah?"

"Recalculating," the GPS says.

"Fuck," I rumble as I slow down and pull over. I do a U-Turn with a sigh.

"Distracted?" Krissy asks softly.

I glance in the rearview mirror. It looks like Raina is out cold. "Yeah, I'm just thinking of my…" I trail off as I catch myself. "Uh… my friend. He's been going through some shit, and with me and Raina being out here, I can't do much to help him. That's a struggle for me." There. That's vague enough to cover both Adam and Jake without me saying more.

"I understand that. Caden said he had some things to take care of and needed me safe." She looks down at her hands. "That worries me."

I make the turn onto the road leading to the cabin, then reach over and pat her thigh. "Caden's a good cop. He knows what he's doing."

"I know he's a good cop. I do. I just… It's hard because he won't tell me what's going on. Just to trust you and Adam."

I glance at her, slightly surprised, before chuckling. "There's no love lost between us and Caden, but he's right. You can trust us. And no matter what our relationship is with him, Caden is a good cop."

She smiles a little. "He's the best husband. The best person. He told me a little about what happened between you all. Not a lot. I know it was a long time ago."

"He can definitely hold a grudge."

"Oh, I think you and Adam can, too."

I laugh. "You got that right."

"Maybe all of this will bring you closer. Like you used to be."

"Maybe. But I'll never get my hopes up about it. Our relationship is dead and gone and buried."

"Maybe there's still a little bit of a pulse there. Maybe it can still be resurrected."

I chuckle. "I hear people talk about you sometimes. I never hear anything other than how sweet you are. Positive. Uplifting." I glance over at her with a smirk as I park the truck in the garage at the cabin we just arrived at. “It’s gross.”

She giggles. “Yes. My optimistic personality is disgusting.”

“So disgusting. Tone it the fuck down.” I playfully roll my eyes as I open the door. Krissy all out laughs and wakes Raina up. I smile at her. “We’re here, sleepy head.”

She wrinkles her nose. “I hate to sound spoiled and entitled, but I miss Bentley and want to see him.”

I open her door as Krissy opens the other one and starts grabbing our suitcases and bags. Killer, their German Shepherd dog, stays glued to Raina. I won’t lie. That makes me feel a fuck of a lot better. Having a second bodyguard for her, for all of us, can’t be a bad thing.

“I know honey. This will all be over soon.”

“It’s been years.”

I’d say she was exaggerating, but as she jumps down, I realize it really has been years. It’s been most of her life.

Killer follows her, pausing to give me a look that I swear says ‘Hurt my new friend, and I’ll tear your balls off’. I inadvertently cover my precious nutsack as he walks past me with his head held high and confidently.

I lean in and pull the rest of the bags out as Krissy wheels her two suitcases towards the garage door. I put my duffel bag and Raina’s over my shoulder and check to make sure nothing is forgotten. I know she had her backpack, so when I don’t see it, I don’t wonder where it went. I close the door and head inside the cabin.

It’s spacious, an open floor plan with a hallway that leads to, what I assume, are bedrooms. Krissy rubs her eyes and turns to me. Raina is standing next to me. Killer is trotting to the kitchen like he owns the place.

He probably does.

“I’d make dinner, but I have to wait until Caden gets here with supplies. I’m sure he’ll bring something if you don’t mind waiting.”

“We don’t mind,” Raina says shyly as she takes a step behind me.

Krissy nods with a soft smile. “Things have been hectic today. I was hoping for a nap. I’ll show you the bedrooms first.” She turns and heads down the hall. Killer looks at us as he follows her. I’m sure that means he wants us to tag along.

I chuckle as we do.

Krissy stops at the first door and turns to us. "We have three bedrooms. The master bedroom, and two guest bedrooms. One of the guest bedrooms has a bathroom and shower. The other doesn't. This first room is the shared bathroom. And this room across from it is the guest bedroom that doesn't have one."

Raina nods and heads for the room without the bathroom. "This one is mine. I know my dad likes having his own bathroom."

I don't get to say anything before Raina is closing the door. I want to comfort her, I know she's upset about all of this and for not being able to see her friends and her boyfriend, but I also know this is Adam's place. And he's way better at it than I am anyway.

"And then this room is the one with the bathroom. The master is down the hall at the end. If you come over here past the guest room, though, there's a hot tub." She moves down the hallway, and I follow. "This is the laundry room. And right out the door is the hot tub and an in-ground pool."

"Oh wow. Nice."

"It was something Caden had installed. He wanted to be sure that when we escaped, it was like going to a luxury spa."

"Well, he's a smart guy. That's definitely how I'd go about it."

She smiles, and for the first time, I can see how tired she is. "Would you mind if I took a nap?" she asks, hopefully.

"No. Don't mind at all. Take a nap. I'll be out in the living room until Caden and Adam get here."

Once she's safely closed behind her door, I make sure all of the doors are locked before I sit on the couch and turn on the TV. I let out a long breath and close my eyes.

I didn't say it out loud, but with there being only one other room, one of us will have to sleep on the couch.

I can't even begin to process how much I *want* to share a room with him…

Chapter Nine

❄ Adam ❄

"I thought I might find you out here," a deep, friendly voice says from behind me.

I raise an eyebrow because that voice doesn't belong to someone who's friendly with me. "What do you want, Caden?" I growl as I skip another rock across the river in front of me. I've been sitting here ever since I kissed Jake this morning.

What the fuck was I thinking?

This is my place of peace. The river running. The animals. The wind through the trees. I'm happy here. It's been my sanctuary ever since I was a kid. I used to climb the same tree I found Raina in just a few weeks ago. I swam in this river with my friends almost every day. This is my space.

"Adam?"

I shake myself out of my thoughts and look at Caden as he sits down. "What? Why are you here?"

"Fuck, something really must be going on in your head if you didn't hear anything I just said."

I reach up and rub my temples. The headache that started on the way here has grown tenfold. "Yeah. But I'm sure you know that."

"What if I said I figured out a whole bunch of stuff and can help you make sure your ex never comes within ten miles of your daughter again?"

I narrow my eyes as I look at him suspiciously. "I'd probably ask you what you're on or if you're drunk."

"Not on anything. Not drunk. I don't have a fuck of a lot of time to explain either, but what if I said Adrian and your daughter are with my wife at my cabin, and to protect you, I need you to come there with me?"

"What do you mean to protect me? And why are they at your cabin?"

"A search warrant is being executed on Adrian's house right now. They're working on one for yours, but it's hard. They used my notes from a conversation I had with my brother. I left them in my locked office last night. This morning, they were gone. Someone had gotten into my office and locked the door behind them. The only person who has keys to my office are people higher up than me. Whoever it was put together a team. I don't think the person leading the team is in on it because he has no access to my office."

"Let me guess. Mateo."

Caden chuckles. "Yeah. I think he's following orders. He doesn't know I had a conversation with my brother. I hadn't had a chance to talk to him before everything went down."

I nod and give him a half smile. Mateo is Caden's best friend. Has been for as long as I can remember. Partners on the field and off. Mateo wouldn't betray Caden, even if it meant his life. Caden is the same way.

And both as big of an asshole as the other.

"Look, Adam. I haven't given you a reason to trust me, but I need you to do it now. The department is going fucking crazy right now. I'm doing some investigating, but I need you, Aiden, and Raina to disappear."

I give him a long look, studying him for the least bit of deception. Finally, I look away and sigh. "I'm sorry about Troy." It's words I never wanted to say but know I've needed to. "I know I hurt him. He didn't deserve that. I was young and dumb and -"

"This isn't about Troy, man. But thank you for the apology. I'm not the one you need to talk to about it, though."

I nod. "Yeah. Yeah, I know."

"I hate to rush you, man, but we need to get to your house and grab your truck. Aiden has mine. I have his bike, but we need to get you some things for a couple of days. I'm really not kidding. I need you to disappear while I figure out who's dirty in my department."

"I feel like this is going to hurt my case."

"I already talked to your attorney. She's expediting the hearing with Raina's statement and some evidence I've collected. She wasn't around you this entire time. You're in the clear."

"What about Adrian?"

"He's harboring a runaway, but I talked to the DA. She's not charging him, but the ADA is going to try. Adrian might get arrested, but the DA won't charge, so there isn't a case. She overrules the ADA and I gave her evidence that he's involved in this whole thing anyway. He'll be arrested very soon."

I nod, trusting him because I'm too fucking worn out not to. "We're going to have one extra person with us." I'm not leaving Jake.

"You talking about Jake Ryan?"

I look down at him as I get up. "Yeah. How'd you know?"

"His case just came across my desk this morning. Stalker?"

"Yeah. It's fucking crazy. No idea who he is. Jake has no idea either. The thing is, I recognized his voice. I just can't place it. I was going to ask Jake about it this morning, but -" I cut myself off. Best not to tell him my lastest fuck up.

Caden stands with a sigh. "I'm assuming he's with you. Staying and on the more intimate side of things. Really with you."

I chuckle. "Always were too smart for your own good."

He chuckles. "I need to talk to him anyway. Let's get the hell out of here before things get worse."

"They can't toss my house if I'm not there to let them in, right?"

"Depends on the warrant. They don't have a no knock, so technically, no. They can't. But if they have a reasonable belief you're inside or the person they're looking for is, yeah. They can enter. All they have to do is articulate they think you're there and give supporting evidence to back it up."

"Which they can lie about."

Caden starts walking towards the road. I follow. "Yeah. They can. There's nothing stopping a cop from lying except morals. Dirty cops don't have 'em. They'll say they saw your vehicle in the garage. An open window. A shade move. Heard a door close. Saw a shadow. As long as they don't fall apart under oath when it goes to court, they can lie all they want. No one would be the wiser."

I shake my head. "Wow. And you wanted in on this? To join the cop ranks?"

"To change the world. Yeah." He smirks. "I had big hopes for my career. And I've done good so far. I haven't run into a situation like this in my department since I've been working for it, but that doesn't mean I have blinders on. I see shit going down in other departments. Bad cops give us good ones a bad name. Bad reputation. We're lumped in with dirty cops because that's what the media portrays. They don't show the good stuff we do. And those that do show the good stuff, no one pays attention. People are wired to see the bad."

I ponder that as we walk. When we reach the bikes, I finally look at him. "Why do you do it?"

It takes him a moment. He climbs on Adrian's bike and grabs his helmet. "For this. Helping people who need it. Taking down the bad guys. The adrenaline rush is nice, but it's the look on the faces of the families or people that I've worked to get justice for that really does it for me. Keeps me going."

He puts the helmet on as I get on my bike. I put my helmet on, and we sync our comms so we can talk on the ride. By the time we near my house, I notice two things. The first is that my garage door is open and truck is gone. The second is that there's a black sedan that I don't recognize sitting brazenly in the open in front my house.

"Hold up," Caden says as we slow. He moves ahead of me, driving by the sedan and pulling into my driveway. The sedan takes off. It takes everything in me not to chase it. "It's not one of ours. The guy was wearing a ski mask."

"Sounds like Jake's stalker to me." I pull in behind him, and we take off the helmets. We park the bikes in the garage."

"Where's your truck?"

"I don't know. Doesn't look like my door was kicked in, so I don't think the department stole it. I left Jake a note saying he could use my truck if he needed it, but that I really didn't want him leaving the house if he could help it unless I was with him."

"Looks like he disobeyed the almighty Adam Damien." Caden smirks as I let us into the house.

"Fuck you," I say with a grin. "I expected this place to be tossed." I look over my shoulder at him. His eyes are on his phone. I push the button to close the garage door.

He shakes his head. "The warrant was denied. They tossed Adrian's place. Found no sign of Raina, so he's in the clear. Arrest warrant is void. My notes from my brother said he'd seen a girl. Didn't confirm it was Raina, but he thought it was. And I put that in there. So the warrant they got for him was definitely pushed."

"We're gonna have to run by there. See if they at least closed the damn door."

"I want to grab his truck anyway. I'll leave his bike here. The more vehicles we have, the better. Just in case we need to leave quick. We'll park the trucks strategically around the property near the doors."

"How many doors you got?"

"Three. Front. Balcony off the master, and there's a side door that goes to the hot tub."

"I feel like the exits were intentional."

"A good cop always has multiple exits and escape routes."

I laugh as I walk up the stairs to my room. "Guess it's a good thing you have a heart after all. Thanks for coming back for me."

Caden just grins as he stays near the window to keep a lookout. I grab enough clothes for a few days. I jog to the bathroom and grab everything else I need. After packing it all in my duffle bag and closing it, I head down the stairs.

"I need to call Jake."

"No need. He just pulled up."

We both walk outside. I lock up my house and turn towards Jake. "We're leaving. Just put that in the truck." I gesture to the duffle back he has slung over his shoulder.

He raises an eyebrow as Caden walks past him to the truck, swiping the keys from his hand on the way by. He starts checking the vehicle for something, I would guess tracking devices, before he climbs in the driver's side. "What's going on?"

"I don't know. But that's Lieutenant Caden Andrews. Something big is going down, and he's getting us the fuck out. He's also the one who has your case. So, it's a win for us both. He's good at what he does. I need you to shut off your phone."

"Okay." Jake turns back the way he came, taking his phone out of his pocket and shutting it off. When we get to my truck, he climbs in the back. I jump in the passenger side.

Caden takes off. "We need to be quick with this. A lot of times, they'll keep surveillance. Be fast with the switch. Be ready to run." He dials someone on his phone and puts it on speaker.

"What's up, Lieutenant?" someone answers.

"Mateo. Did you leave anyone at Sloan's place?"

"Yeah. I have patrol there until I can get back there."

"Get rid of them. Give me two minutes. Tell them to go get coffee."

"You got it. What's going on?"

"Call me later. Can't talk now. Just need you to trust me. Who gave you this case?"

"Joseph Danvis."

Caden scoffs. "Fucking figures."

"I texted patrol. Told him to grab a coffee. He said okay. He's in a marked squad."

It doesn't take long to get to Adrian's house. When Caden gets to the corner where he needs to turn, the patrol car is pulling away. Caden waits until he turns the corner and is out of sight before he makes his move. He pulls into the driveway. We both jump out. Jake stays in the truck but moves to the front seat. I love that he does what I need him to without me telling him to.

I push away the thoughts that invade my mind as I run to the front door, Caden on my heels. Adrian has a combination box hidden above his door that has an extra key. My hope is that his spare key to his truck is still hanging on the hook where it belongs. Adrian is meticulous about keeping keys in one place so they don't get lost.

Once I get the key out, I open the door. I put the key back and the lockbox right where it belongs. We enter the house. I'm taken aback at the mess from the search, but his keys are where they should be. I lock the house door from the inside. We enter the garage from inside the house. Caden checks the truck, underneath and everything, just like he did mine. He jumps in Adrian's truck after I hand him the key and he's done with his check. I open the garage. Caden quickly exits. I close it and duck under the door. I jog to my truck and jump in the driver's side.

I don't breathe until we're on the open highway heading out of Piper Falls. I'm hyperaware that Jake is right next to me, but I can't talk to him. Can't ease his mind. Not until I know we're safe and not being followed.

"Does this have to do with my stalker?" Jake asks after we've been driving for a while.

"I don't know. Caden didn't give me a lot of information, but I have a feeling it has more to do with me than you." I glance at him. His eyes haven't left his feet the entire time we've been driving. I want to reach over and take his hand; squeeze his thigh… Anything to give him a little comfort; ease his fears.

But I can't. Instead, I grip the steering wheel tighter. My jaw ticks. I glance at him again and notice he's grinding his teeth. He has to be. His jaw is moving in a manner that proves my suspicions.

"Jake, please don't. Don't clench your jaw. Don't grind your teeth. It'll only hurt you and give you a headache."

He lets out a humorless laugh. "Already there."

I swallow because I don't know if he means he's hurt by my kissing his soul out of him and then leaving, or if he means he already has a headache.

Or both.

"Where did you go earlier?" I ask, trying to change the subject.

"I figured you didn't want me to leave your house, but I needed clothes. I didn't know where you went or when you were coming back, so I went to get some clothes. I promised Henry I'd have lunch with him and play cards. So I did that. I was on my way back to your house, but then realized I needed to get my shifts covered. So, I went there and then back to your house. You were there then. I was gone a few hours, probably."

I nod. "Somewhere in there, your stalker showed back up. He was sitting outside my house, so I'm glad I got there when I did. I chased him away. Did you leave the garage door open?"

"No." He shakes his head. "I closed it."

I nod again. "I'll have to take a look at the security cameras. It was open when I got there."

Jake falls silent again. Not like he was talking loudly in the first place. He sounds defeated, and that breaks every fiber of my being. The feeling of reaching for him becomes overwhelming, but I don't want to give him false hope. He deserves better than me. A lot better. I'm not even sure he really knows who I am anyway. That I'm really BloodKnight. That BloodKnight is me.

"I'm sorry I'm not good enough," Jake whispers under his breath.

I swallow so hard that my chest hurts. I grip the steering wheel even tighter so I don't pull him close to me and tell him he's wrong. It's not the time or place.

But I won't fucking let him believe that for long. As soon as we get to the cabin, I'm sitting him down and having a long talk. I'll come clean about who I am and everything. I'll explain that me not being able to give him what he needs and wants is on me, not him.

You're good enough, Jake, I think to myself, swallowing around the lump in my throat. *Too good for me.*

Chapter Ten

The moment we get to the cabin, it feels like utter pandemonium is unleashing around me. Like the gates of hell have actually opened, and we're all clinging to whatever we can to stay above ground.

But what's the point? It seems like everyone's life is in shambles anyway. May as well give into the inevitable and pick out my corner in the depths of eternal damnation.

All of us are without phones. We all had them shut off, but Caden has gone one step further and taken them all. Better safe than sorry. That's what he told us. Everything else he said makes it seem like we aren't safe at all. I've got a stalker. Adrian and Adam have dirty cops after them. It's the makings of a fucking movie.

A horror movie.

One without a happy ending where everyone dies.

"Jake?" Caden's voice cuts through my dark thoughts.

I run my fingers through my hair with a long sigh. "Sorry. This is a lot."

"I know," Caden agrees. "But I promise you're safe here. There were no tracking devices on the trucks. I checked. Phones are off. We weren't followed. But I need to know if you can think of anyone who would be after you like this."

I slowly look down at my hands while I shrug. I've been thinking of that voice. I know it. I'm pretty sure I've pinned it down, but it doesn't make sense.

Or maybe it does. BloodKnight and TraumaBull are here in Piper Falls. What if *he* is, too?

I shake my head. It can't be. It just can't. "None that I can think of. All I do is work. I can't think of anyone I've messed up the order for who would want me dead." I try to give a brave smile to show I'm kidding, but I can't muster it. I'm exhausted.

And I can't stop thinking about the ride over here. Or the entire day for that matter. Why did Adam kiss me like that and then run? It was like I burned him or something. He couldn't get away fast enough. And there I was left wondering what the fuck even happened.

The conversation drones on around me, but I can't focus. Adam hasn't left his daughter's side. Raina keeps wiping tears. Caden's wife hasn't said a word. Adrian is on the couch on the other side of Raina. I'm sitting on the loveseat.

Alone.

Like a leper.

Fuck. Fuck all of this.

I stand in the middle of whatever Caden is talking about. "Look, I'm sorry, but I'm not feeling the best. I'm just gonna head to the bedroom." I quickly make my exit.

Once I reach the bedroom, I close the door and lean my back against it. I close my eyes and let out a long breath. I'm sharing a room with Aiden and Adam. There's a nice, comfy looking chair in the corner that I've claimed as my bed. It's out of the way. I won't bother anyone there or get in trouble. I seem to be good at both of those things.

I let out another breath as I open my eyes. I rub my head and eyes as I head for the chair. I don't bother changing into my sleep pants. I just stay in my clothes. My long sleeve black shirt hides my arms nicely. My shoes are out by the front door. Krissy doesn't like shoes in the house. I don't blame her. She's a very clean person and shoes track a lot of dirt.

I grab the blanket laying out for me and sit down in the chair. I try to shut off my mind, but it wanders and makes pit stops in territory I don't want anything to do with. Like how much better everyone's life would be if I didn't have a stalker making things harder. Adam has enough going on with his daughter. Adrian is just as involved because he's been hiding Raina. Caden has to deal with dirty cops in the department and worrying who he can and can't trust. And poor Krissy is just thrust into this mess.

I sigh and switch to my side. My legs are on a big ottoman. I'm pretty tall, but the chair and ottoman fit me well. I knew it would be comfortable, but honestly, I could sleep anywhere.

When my mind isn't fighting it.

❄❄❄

When I wake up, I hear hushed voices. I didn't know I even fell asleep. I blink my eyes a few times, but I'm comfortable, so I don't want to move yet.

"It just broke me, man. He deserves better," one of the voices says. I think it's Adam, but I'm not completely awake.

"He's more than good enough," another voice says. I'm starting to wake up more and more. I know that one is Adrian.

I still don't move, though. It's rude to eavesdrop, but I want to know what they're talking about.

And who…

"I don't think he knows I heard him say it, but his words just keep roaring through my head. And his fucking shattered voice when he said it. I could tell he was broken. I know it's my fault. I know it's because I left after kissing him, but… Fuck, I messed up. I should've at least said something. Or just reached over and touched him. Anything."

There's silence for a few moments. I feel tears sting my eyes because I know they're talking about me now. And he's right. I really do feel broken. Not good enough.

"You guys can stop talking about me," I mumble as I sit up. I raise an eyebrow because I know I'm not in the chair anymore. "Why am I in the bed?"

"Because we're not letting you sleep in the fucking chair," Adrian says.

"I'm really fine sleeping in the chair," I snap as I get up.

"You may be fine sleeping in the chair, but we're not letting you. You looked uncomfortable as fuck." Adam's eyes follow me to the door. "Where are you going?"

I roll my eyes. "The bathroom. Unless that's off limits, too." I know there's a bathroom in here, but I need a minute to calm down.

"Jake. Knock it off," Adrian warns, his voice low and gravelly.

"Make me," I grumble under my breath as I leave the room.

I duck into the bathroom and do what I need to. The house is silent. I have no idea what time it is, but it must be the middle of night. It's really dark outside. It's darkest before dawn, right? Isn't that the saying?

After washing my hands, I walk back to the room. I close the door and head straight towards the chair, but I'm blocked by Adam. He folds his arms over his chest and gives me a look that both makes my dick hard and sends shivers of fear through my entire soul.

"You're not sleeping on the chair," Adam growls.

I give him a death stare of my own. "And who are you to force me to sleep where I don't want to? You already made it pretty clear you don't want me. I'm not good enough for you, right?" Before Adam gets a chance to respond, I'm launched into his solid chest. My ass stings. I reach for it as I right myself and stare in disbelief at Adrian.

"Do you need TraumaBull and BloodKnight?" Adrian asks, his voice just as dangerous as Adam's. I swallow. Hard. "You seem to listen pretty well to them, don't you? Little sub?"

My mouth goes instantly dry. I forget how to speak. He's not wrong. If they told me to do something, I obeyed without hesitation or thought. Because I am their little sub. Which means…

They've confirmed what I knew.

I lower my eyes, submissively, my body leading the way. I drop to my knees and let my hands fall open-palmed and facing up onto my lap. It might look to most like I've given up, but to me, it feels natural. It feels like I'm giving up control that I don't want anyway to the two men standing above me. I have to play the tough one with a thick skin whenever I'm working. I play the well put together guy when I'm at Henry's because I want him to feel taken care of.

But then I go home. Alone. I turn on WOW. I follow orders. Orders given by these two. And nothing has ever felt more natural to me. More real. It's a fictional world, but it's the only place I get to let go and be myself. It's the only place I can fall and know I'll be caught.

Just like now.

Adam's index and middle finger cup my chin. Adrian's hand runs through my hair and tugs. I look up at them both, my head back, my neck bared. I'd do anything they asked of me, and they know it.

"You're not sleeping on the chair," Adrian rumbles. I can hear the dominance of TraumaBull seeping from his throat.

"We'd both sleep on the floor before we allowed you to sleep on a fucking chair," Adam growls, BloodKnight bubbling to the surface.

This is what I needed.

It's what I wanted.

Them.

It's always going to be them.

Adam lets go of my jaw and holds a hand out to me. Adrian lets go of my hair and does the same. Keeping my eyes on both of them, I reach up and put my hands in their outstretched ones. They pull me to my feet and back me to the bed, pushing me onto it.

"Take off your shirt," Adam commands. I do so without hesitation.

Adrian takes it from me and tosses it as he puts one knee on the bed next to me. He's not caging me in, yet, but it feels like it. Two large and muscular men on each side of me makes me feel like I'm trapped, but I don't want to run. I'm right where I want to be.

"Lay down." Adrian's deep voice reverberates through my entire soul. My body obeys like it needs the commands to survive.

On the bed, Adam and Adrian sit on their knees. Starting from the top of my head, they both start exploring my body with their large and well-worked hands, moving down… down… When they reach my stomach, they take an excruciating amount of time tracing my abs. I find myself breathing heavier; faster, whimpering for them to not stop while simultaneously praying to every entity that exists for them to keep going lower.

I don't need to look to see I'm dangerously close to poking through my jeans. It's painful. I want to reach down and allow my dick to spring free, but I don't dare move. I don't want them to stop.

Adam's hand stops just above the waistband of my jeans. Adrian's follow. Adam's eyes meet mine while Adrian's focus on the tent forming in my jeans. I gasp and arch slightly, silently begging them to touch me more.

For the first time, I don't hear the voice in the back of my head saying I need to be punished. I don't think about my arms and what they show of the dark world I try so hard to hide.

"I need you to say yes or no. Understand?" Adam asks. I nod because I can't speak. "Are you okay with us touching your dick?" Adam licks his lower lip as he watches me intently. Adrian grips my waistband. I nod again.

Adrian shakes his head. "No. Say it. Verbalize yes or no to us. We aren't continuing without that consent. Be a good boy for us."

My eyes are wide. My heart is beating out of my chest, but I manage the words. "Yes… Oh, fuck yes, please." Them asking for consent is a lot sexier than I ever thought it could be.

Adam's grin makes my heart stop. My cock gets harder, but just before I start begging, Adam flicks the button on my jeans open. Adrian holds my hard length down with one hand while pulling my zipper down with the other. Every movement makes me jerk. My dick twitches. I suck in sharp breaths as I watch them.

Adam tugs my pants and underwear down. When my cock pops out, Adrian's hands are on it faster than I can register what's going on. His hands are warm. Rough. He strokes, slow, his chiseled face turning towards mine. He grins a sexy smirk, and I'm gone.

But it's Adam that renders me paralyzed. His tongue hits my tip. He licks the bead of precome already seeping out of me. I forget how to breathe. My chest stops rising and falling. I grip the sheets as my mouth falls open.

Adrian tugs my balls with one hand as he strokes with other. Adam sucks my tip into his mouth. I arch up and moan loudly as my eyes roll back in my head. I suck in a huge gulp of air when my lungs start burning. My dick becomes thicker. I'm going to come, and I'm not going to be able to stop it.

Adam shifts, his tongue still lashing my tip as he sucks, and slaps one of his large hands over my mouth. "You need to be quiet, baby."

I nod and arch into the strokes, fucking both Adrian's hand and Adam's mouth. Still playing with my balls, Adrian stops stroking and replaces his hand with his tongue. He licks up my length. He sucks and nibbles along my vein. Adam's hand remains on my mouth, muffling my whimpers, moans, and cries. I'm so happy and simultaneously overwhelmed that tears are streaming from the corners of my eyes. I arch up again, needing to feel more of them, when Adam's hand slides down my ass. As my body is about to hit the bed again, his wet finger slides in. I scream out, my eyes wide, and come.

Hard.

In Adam's mouth.

I feel some of my come, or maybe it's Adam's spit, drip down my twitching cock onto Adrian. Adam's finger twitches in my hole. He hits something that has me coming again. Though, I don't know if it's really a second time, or if he just retriggered what was already happening.

I'm sweating.

Panting.

My body is twitching as I try to catch my breath.

Adam is milking my cock for everything I have and more.

And all the while, Adrian's tongue is licking me, sucking my length, rolling my balls in his palm, and swallowing everything Adam let escape down my shaft.

As I'm coming down, Adam removes his hand from my mouth as he's slowly removing his finger from my tight pucker. His mouth pops off my cock. Adrian licks me clean as my body trembles. I feel like I'm going in and out of consciousness. Stars are still exploding in front of my eyes. When they fall closed, all I can see is gold fireworks.

I don't remember falling asleep, but when I wake up, a strong pair of arms are wrapped tightly around me. It's still completely dark in the room. I turn my head slightly to see Adrian's beautiful silhouette. He moves just a little, but his arms tighten around me even more. I smile, unsure if I'm dreaming. I pinch myself and smile wider when I feel it. I curl into him even more, my rear pushing into his gorgeous length.

But something's missing.

Rather, someone.

Adam.

I look around the room the best I can, but don't see him.

Just like that, as I sink further into Adrian, I'm flooded with thoughts of not being good enough. Of doing something wrong to push him away. I try to fight the thoughts, but sleep doesn't come easy.

I need another punishment... I'll cut deeper this time... He'd be happier if I left this world...

I reach up and wipe away tears.

They'd both be better off without me.

Chapter Eleven

❄ Adrian ❄

When I wake up, it's still dark. Jake pushes back into me. I tighten my grip around him when I feel him try and get up. I know he's looking for Adam.

But Adam left the room after Jake fell asleep, mumbling something about fucking up again. I sighed but didn't try to stop him this time. He obviously needs time to figure things out, but I'm not letting him get back into his damn head. We had a breakthrough tonight. He let me kiss him while I was licking Jake and he was sucking him off. I'm not fucking willing to give it up.

Jake is restless.

It feels like hours before I finally soothe him to sleep with a back rub. The sun is coming up, but he needs sleep. I heard him sniffling a few times, and it broke me. I know Adam is hurting him. Not intentionally, but it's happening.

And I can't allow it. I can't allow Adam to keep hurting himself or Jake.

Or me.

Jake's nails dig into my arm. He's been holding it like a teddy bear for a while now. I'm feeling pins and needles, but no way in hell I'm moving. He makes whimpering noises before he starts trembling. Instead of gripping me, he scratches.

I hug him even tighter, pressing my lips against his neck. "Shh... baby. I'm right here. I'm not going anywhere."

I wince when the scratch deepens. I don't want to wake him, but I have to. I kiss his neck, trying to stir him gently. It doesn't work. He's drawing blood now, and he's starting to sweat. I don't care about the pain. It's him going through whatever hell he's experiencing in his mind that bothers me.

I look up when the door quietly opens. Adam's eyes widen when mine meet his. I have to look a little wild. Desperate.

I do what I can and just hug Jake harder so he knows I'm here. Adam sits down on the bed. He puts his hand on Jake's thigh and squeezes. Jake's still shaking, but his grip on me loosens. I still don't move my arm.

Adam leans down, his hand still on Jake's thigh. He kisses his forehead and looks me directly in the eyes. "We're both here, sunshine. You're safe. Everything's going to be okay now. I'm not going anywhere."

I know he's talking to me just as much as Jake. Adam runs his fingers through Jake's hair as he moves his other hand from Jake's thigh to mine. His eyes never leave mine, just as his lips never leave Jake's forehead. Adam lays down with Jake between us and hugs us both. I didn't realize my heart was racing so badly until I let out a breath of relief.

We lay like that for several hours. Adam and I both doze off, but neither of us do it at the same time. Instinctively, we know that Jake needs one of us to be awake if he starts having a nightmare again. So, while Jake sleeps peacefully, Adam and I keep watch over him and each other...

After a restless night and really boring day, the three of us are sitting in the hot tub after a swim. The silence is deafening. The tension could be shot with a Glock. The bullet wouldn't pierce through. Jake hasn't said a word all day. He wouldn't tell either of us what he dreamed, but he can't take his eyes off the scratches on my arm. I've tried to tell him that I'm okay. They don't hurt. He doesn't believe me.

"Jake. Talk to us," Adam finally says, breaking the awkward silence. He's not the only one who needs to talk, though. We all do.

Jake keeps his eyes on the water. His hand makes swirling motions. Instead of saying anything, he just shrugs. I can see the change in Adam. He doesn't like shrugging. He takes it as disrespectful. But his look isn't one of dominance and control.

It's of pain.

Like he finally just figured something out. Something I'm not even sure I've managed to.

He moves in front of Jake and lowers himself to his knees. I can see Adam's hands move up Jake's thighs. When they stop half way, Jake finally looks up. I can see the hurt. The red eyes.

Tears.

"Why? Why am I not enough? I just want to know. And then I'll leave you alone. You'll never see or hear from me again. I'll… I'll be gone. Forever." His head drops again, and I finally understand.

"Oh fuck," I whisper as I move to his side. "Your dream. You were…" I trail off. I can't say the words. I don't want to be right.

"Jake," Adam whispers. "You're enough. You're more than enough. I need you to know that."

"But you keep leaving." Jake's voice quivers. I glare at Adam as I put my arm around Jake.

Adam nods. "I know. But baby, that had nothing to do with you. It's all me. I know how stupid and cliche that sounds, but it's the truth. You're not to blame for my actions. I ran because I was scared. Scared because I know I'm not worthy of you. You're way too good, and I've made a lot of mistakes. Kissing you, being with you, that all taints you and your innocence." Adam cups Jake's jaw and makes him look at him. "I never want to be the one who destroys that."

Jake's mouth opens but closes again. He crosses his arms over his chest and nods. I know he's shutting down. Closing himself off.

And that's when I see it. The confirmation of what I think his dream was about.

Before I have a chance to do anything, though, Adam is already taking Jake's hands in his. He turns them so Jake's palms are up. I tear up because the immense pain I'm seeing in front of my very own eyes is not something I was prepared for.

And some of the cuts look fresh.

Adam leans down and kisses each scar on Jake's arms. When he sits back up, I throw my arms around Jake and kiss his neck.

"Fuck, Jake. I'm so fucking sorry. I'm sorry I didn't see it."

"I'm good at hiding it," he whispers to me, his voice cracking.

Adam stays in front of him holding his hands. "What I said about this all being on me, it doesn't mean I'm going anywhere. I meant what I said. I'm here. I'm not going anywhere. I'm not running anymore. The reason… uh…" Adam clears his throat. "The reason I left this morning, Jake, is because I saw the fresh cuts. I knew they were caused by me. I don't know when you did them. Seeing them hurt me, but it was the wakeup call I needed. I needed to fully grasp your pain in order to see that my feelings for you outweigh the feeling I have about myself not being adequate for you."

His words cut deep. Hearing him say them to me is one thing. We share everything. But he doesn't share everything with anyone else. He's closed off unless he's close to the person. He's not close to anyone but me. Seeing him open up to Jake… it has me choking up because it means that he wants to make this work.

He wants Jake to heal and feel the love he deserves.

He wants us all to.

"Your dream…" I start. "It… you were cutting yourself."

Jake looks down at the water but leans into me. I know he needs comfort, so I hug him as hard as I can. Adam squeezes his hands and runs his thumb over the top of them comfortingly. Jake rests his head on my shoulder as he takes a deep breath.

"It… started when I was young. Not deep. Just… enough to feel it but not leave scars. I was probably like ten. I knew I was different. I'd had my first crush on one of my friends, who had a crush on a girl in our glass. I was jealous about it. I talked to my parents. I was honest. I was confused. I got the beating of my life. After that, every time I had a thought about him that I couldn't shake, I cut my arm. It helped. At least I thought it did. I guess looking back, it really didn't. The feelings never stopped. The cutting continued. When I got kicked out at seventeen, I was homeless. I got a job. I put myself through community college. But the feelings were still there. I was just too busy trying to support myself to cut. I haven't done it in a long time."

"You just started again," Adam whispers, his eyes getting a little watery. His hands squeeze Jake's as I hug him harder. Jake nods, but says nothing.

"Baby, love is love. It doesn't matter who you have eyes for. Unless it's for someone under eighteen. Then there's an issue, but that's not the point. The point is, we might live in the Bible Belt. There might be a lot of bullshit that comes with that. Friends and family pitted against each other, but that's something that happens everywhere. Everyone is entitled to their own beliefs." I pull away just enough to cup his cheek and turn his head so he looks at me. "Just like everyone is entitled to live their own lives. What you went through with your parents is fucked up. It happens to so many, but we can't control them and their beliefs and actions. All we can control is our own beliefs and actions, right?"

He gives a soft smile as he nods. "Right."

Adam grins and leans in closer, his lips close to Jake's. "Who you choose to be with and, ultimately, love is completely up to you. It's your business. No one else's. If you choose to love a lamp, I'd question your sanity, but say, 'Hey. Love is love'."

This gets a chuckle out of Jake that sounds like the greatest melody I've ever heard. I love his laugh. He glances at us both and starts to hug us but hesitates. "And if I'm in love with two people?"

I shrug with a grin. "What about it?"

"That's frowned upon in society."

Adam laughs. "Baby, so is being gay. Yet there's hundreds of thousands of us. Some are bi with a male and female partner. And some are in love with chandeliers. Or ghosts."

Jake straight out laughs. "Where are you even getting this shit?"

I laugh as Adam grins. "Probably from the tabloids."

Adam shakes his head. "Read about it in the *Daily Mail* or something."

"So… the UK. That sounds like a UK thing," I say.

"Why does all this crazy shit happen in the UK?" Jake asks, cracking up.

"Not a clue, sunshine. But it proves my point." Adam leans in the last few inches and kisses Jake. The moan he lets out under his breath when Adam's lips meet his makes me want to devour both of them.

Jake's arms snake around us both. I'm instantly on fire and hard, but I focus on Jake's needs. He needs to be held and reassured. Hell, so do I.

After a few minutes of just holding each other and relishing in the feeling of being close, we pull away, but still remain tightly together. Adam sits on the other side of Jake.

"So how does this work?" I ask. "I know how I want it to work, but how is it going to actually work?"

Jake nods. "I was wondering that, too."

"Well, first thing. No more cutting," Adam's voice is deep and commanding as he watches Jake closely.

"No more cutting," Jake repeats, meeting Adam's eyes. He turns to me. "Promise." His words send much needed comfort through my system. I don't feel like my heart is vibrating anymore.

"As for everything else, I guess I want to say just let it be and see how it goes, but I know that's not how either of you work. So, both of you tell me. What do you need? What do you want?"

I glance at Jake before I speak. "I just want the three of us together. With Jake's stalker, I don't think he should be at his apartment. I think we should be together."

"I agree," Jake whispers. "Not just because of my stalker, though." He takes a deep breath and looks up, his eyes fixed on the house. "I just don't want to waste time. I know that sounds dumb considering my age, but I've learned that waiting for stuff just causes more issues most of the time. If you want it, get it. And… I think we all are on the same page with wanting it."

Adam nods. "If that's what you want, that's what you get. Right, Aiden?"

"Absolutely. I need to figure out what to do with my house, though."

"Keep it. In case it… well, you know." Jake shrugs again.

"If you shrug one more time, sunshine," Adam begins, "I'm taking you over my knee."

Jake's eyes widen as his head snaps towards Adam. "Wha... What?"

"Rule number one. Cutting or hurting yourself with words or anything else, unless it's an accident, will result in five spankings and affirmations. I will absolutely make you sit in front of a mirror for hours repeating whatever I think will help you feel better about yourself. Rule number two. I don't tolerate disrespect. Shrugging. Eye rolling. Both a big no that will result in five spankings. Rule number three. Taking care of yourself. Hygiene. Food. Don't neglect yourself. Rule number four. No lying. I catch you, it's five spankings and no release for a week. I will tease you. I'll let Adrian tease you. But you will not get release. And rule number five. No intentionally putting yourself in danger. Leaving without one of us with a stalker on your heels would fall under that. Same punishment. Five spankings. No release. Questions?"

Jake's eyes are still wide. I smirk as he processes. After a few moments, he shakes his head like he's coming out of some daze. "Yeah. I mean no. No questions. No questions, sir."

"Good boy," Adam says. I love when he pulls out the Alpha card and controls everything. "Houses and apartments. I want you to get out of yours, Jake. Just for the safety purposes. Your stalker knows where you live. It's dangerous. My house is bigger. We can all stay there. Adrian, I want you to keep your house, though. If for no other reason than for Raina to have a place when she turns eighteen."

"Shit, that's a good idea. I was thinking of just selling it or something. It's paid off, but that would be a great thing for Raina. She can focus on school. And if she sticks here, then she'll have her own place."

"She wants to go to Harvard for law, but a place for her to come home to on breaks would be great."

"And I talked to her a bit," Jake offers. "She wants to come here after school and open her own firm. Having her own place to live when she's done with school would be something she doesn't have to worry about."

I grin. "I have no attachment to that house at all. I don't have an issue giving it up. I think that's a great idea, but we'd have to do some expansion to yours. I'm pretty in love with this hot tub, and I want a pool. And the garage needs to be bigger."

Adam laughs. "Anything you want if it means you stay with me. Forever."

"Is this too fast?" Jake asks.

"Not to me," I answer. "But I've known Adam a long time. Does it feel uncomfortable for you? Too quick?"

Jake is silent for a few moments before he shakes his head. "No. I think it feels good. A good pace. Maybe that's crazy."

We all fall into a comfortable silence and sit with each other. Jake is absolutely right. It does feel like a good pace.

It feels right.

Like a piece that's been missing has finally been filled.

Chapter Twelve

(Two Weeks Later)

Sitting behind this cold wooden desk is exactly how I wanted to spend my Monday morning. For weeks, I've been accused of being a kidnapper, of harboring a runaway. I was arrested when I had to go into town from the cabin and take care of some things on site of my current restoration project. My attorney had me out fast, but it's the principal. It never should've happened.

My attorney is droning on and on about the case in legal jargon I won't pretend to understand. I keep my eyes straight ahead. I don't look at Carmen or her dick of an attorney, Richard, Ric for short. Should be Dick because that's what he is. I'm pretty sure she found this guy in a Crackerjack box. Or maybe my attorney is just making this fuck look like an idiot.

"To conclude, your honor, the child has stated, under oath, that she wants to be with her father. She is sixteen-years-old, which makes it legal for her to give her preference for the parent she wants to live with. The courts must take that into consideration. Mr. Damien is a well-reputed and well-respected man in this community who runs charity events throughout the year and a rather large one at Christmas. His program has been proven over and over again to keep kids busy and out of trouble. Furthermore, we have given mounds of evidence proving that Ms. Quinn has been involved with drugs and prostitution. We have evidence supporting child neglect. The DA has charges pending against her for a multitude of things. The ADA has been arrested for being involved in things unbecoming of a man who is supposed to uphold the law. The child will be testifying in the case against her mother and the ADA. But above and beyond all of that, we have a father here who has proven he loves his daughter, and a daughter who feels the same. We've proven the restraining order is based on such blatantly false allegations. These two deserve to be together. They've missed so much time, and should not be forced by the courts to miss more."

"I'm inclined to agree, Ms. Rivera," the judge says. He turns to Carmen and her attorney. "Ms. Quinn is hereby ordered to sign over and relinquish all custody to Mr. Damien, effective immediately. Ms. Quinn must show major improvement before she is allowed any kind of visitation rights, which will be supervised. Ms. Quinn must come to the courts to make this request, and there will be another hearing. Mr. Damien isn't requesting child support at this time, but can in the future, if he so chooses, by coming back to this court."

As the judge continues on, I glance over at Carmen. She's staring straight ahead, but she looks defeated. Like she just lost everything but doesn't dare fight it anymore. I can't really blame her. I showed up with a force today. And my attorney gave hers absolutely no leeway whatsoever. It also helped that we aren't in front of the same asshole judge. We had evidence of that guy getting paid off by Carmen. My attorney is fucking incredible.

By the time the judge dismisses us, Carmen still hasn't moved an inch. I have nothing to say to her, so I leave the courtroom with my attorney. Jake and Adrian are close behind us. Caden and Mateo are behind them. Raina is in a separate room. She broke down earlier during her testimony, so she was brought to a private room where she could take time to relax. I was afraid to even take her here because I thought the second they saw her with me, I'd be arrested on the spot. Instead, I was met by my attorney and a counselor. The counselor is who Raina is with right now.

The last couple of weeks have been fucking insane. Caden and Mateo uncovered an entire trafficking ring that went right up to top city officials. By the time he figured it all out and brought it all to the mayor, the department itself had been shaken to its core. The chief of police himself was involved. The deputy mayor. Even the city manager. Caden and Mateo uncovered a huge scandal. The FBI had gotten involved and quietly arrested several people in Piper Falls and throughout Texas. It made national headlines and was quickly forgotten about. Goes to show the desensitization of the world.

I made my peace with Troy. Caden asked his brothers to take turns being at the cabin with us when he was at work. The first day Troy was there, I sat down and had a long conversation with him. There were a few tears, some hugs, and a lot of heartfelt emotions. By the time it was over, we both felt a lot better about things. Troy is able to move on. We've even become friends again.

Once we get out of the courtroom, Raina is running to me. I catch her and hug her hard. Her tears, I hope of happiness, soak my neck. I'm unwilling to let her go. Even though she's been with me up at the cabin, the tension and stress she's been under has been killing me.

My hope is that with all of this being over, she'll be able to get back to her funloving self and not feel afraid of someone coming after her to drag her back to her mom.

My intention was to have Jake sit between me and Adrian while we settled to watch *Haunting in Connecticut*. I didn't expect that I'd be the one in the middle soaking in all the cuddles. But damn if being spoiled by the men I'm so deeply in love with doesn't give me warm fuzzies.

When Bentley, Raina's boyfriend, stopped by to see her, the fuzzies got fuzzier. She looks so happy cuddled into his side. So calm and relaxed. She deserves that and so much more. We all deserve that. And I'm going to make sure we all get it.

The movie is halfway through. Raina's head is on Bentley's chest. Jake is gripping my sweats in a very controversial place. Adrian is holding my hand and grinning like an idiot. His favorite thing in the world is horror movies.

There are a couple pizza boxes with a few slices of pizza on the coffee table in front of us. Open sodas and candy. And we could never forget the popcorn with crushed up Heath Crunch candy bars. I can't watch a movie without it.

"I love this part," Adrian says.

"Tell me when it's over," Jake mumbles into my chest.

I kiss his head. "You're not a horror movie kind of guy, are you?"

"Give me *Chucky*. Give me *The Shining*. But this 'based on real events' shit ain't it for me." Jake jumps a little when the kid in the movie sees someone. "Fuck this." He hides his head back in my chest. I can't say I mind it at all. I just wrap him up tighter and hug him closer.

"Ooh! Can we watch Stephen King's *The Mist* after this one?" Raina asks.

I grin. "One of my favorites. Absolutely."

"I do like that one a lot," Jake chips in. "But I'm hiding until we put that one on."

"Fair enough." Adrian reaches over and gives Jake's arm a squeeze.

Once the movie is over, we all take a minute to stretch. We refill the snacks and drinks and each take more pizza as we settle for our second movie.

"This is nice," Bentley says as he wraps Raina in a blanket before hugging her tight to him. "I really missed you."

"I missed you, too," Raina says softly as she looks up at him adoringly.

I can't help the grin that spreads across my face as I grab another blanket for me, Jake, and Adrian. They've, once again, left me the seat in the middle. I shake my head. "Not this time. Jake, get in the middle."

Jake looks at me wide-eyed before his gaze darts to Adrian like he's pleading for help. I almost laugh, but don't. Instead, I narrow my eyes dominantly.

Adrian shakes his head. "Not a chance. We're pampering you tonight. Sit down so we can finish what we started."

My mouth opens, then closes. I sit as I chuckle and spread the blanket around the three of us. Raina starts the movie, and I find myself relaxing completely for the first time in a very, very long time. The tension I've been carrying seemingly releases. My aching shoulders and neck loosen. My chest that always feels tight releases. I let out a long sigh as my eyes close.

"You okay?" Adrian whispers.

I give him a genuine half smile, keeping my eyes shut. "Yeah. Yeah, I'm good. I feel good for the first time in a while. Content."

"Good. That's the point of you being in the middle."

My half smile turns into a full one as I open my eyes and look at him. "Thank you. For literally everything. Putting up with me. Helping with Raina and putting your own life and freedom at risk. I don't know what I'd do without you."

"Good thing you'll never have to find out."

"Good thing." I hug Jake closer to me and kiss his head. "I'm glad you stuck around for me, too."

Jake smiles up at me and squeezes my thigh. My dick twitches, and I'm glad I'm under the covers. I can feel it growing. "I wouldn't want to be anywhere else."

The movie begins, and I'm instantly engrossed. *The Mist* is such a good movie. The right amount of horror and psychological thriller combine to make it the perfect level of chaos and mayhem with an ending that has anyone wondering what just happened and why. Heartstopping and heartwrenching all at once.

Near the end of the movie, Raina meets my eyes and smiles. I grin back and wink.

Then watch her face turn from purely happy to undeniably terrified in point two seconds flat.

Alarmed, I follow her eyes just as she starts screaming.

My eyes meet the coldest dark depths I've ever seen in my life. Coal black eyes stare back at me, but not at *me.*

At Jake.

I'm on my feet and barking orders before the masked clad man has a second to react. "Jake, take Raina and Bentley to the bathroom! Go!"

"What the fuck is happening?" Adrian asks as he jumps up with me. He's always been my ride or die. Always right with me even if he has no fucking idea what's going on.

"Masked man in the window staring right at Jake."

"Jesus Christ," Adrian murmurs as we both run outside in just socks. "There!" He points to a man running towards a car. He's dressed all in black and has something black covering his head.

We both take off after him. "Stop!" I shout. The man glances over his shoulder and takes off running through a neighbor's yard. Adrian and I both follow.

"Stop, motherfucker!" Adrian orders. The yard is filled with toys that we have to be sure to step over. It doesn't help that they guy is throwing other obstacles in our way. Chairs. Pool noodles. Anything he can get his hands on.

It doesn't stop us. It barely slows us down. We keep on his heels. He's just barely out of arm's reach. Just as he gets to a fence to jump, I lunge for him. I miss by millimeters. He jumps over. Adrian starts to follow, but I stop him.

"Dogs. Their dogs will take care of him. Leave it. Let's go." I pull him by the arm away from the fence. We head back to the house as dogs bark viciously behind us. There's a whimper and a loud scream before I hear yelling.

"Fuck, I wish we could call the cops," Adrian says.

"No point. He got away. He was wearing a mask. No way to identify him."

"Yeah there is. He has a spider tattoo on his hand. And when he jumped the fence, I saw a tattoo of Tails from Sonic. It was color and he was laying down. Like across the lower back."

"I was too busy trying to catch him. I didn't see it. I'm glad you did."

"I want to get my phone and call the police. Report this."

"We'll call Caden or Mateo. They know what's going on."

Aiden and I jog the rest of the way back to the house. When we get there, I'm shocked to see a squad car sitting in my driveway. I glance at Aiden, and we both start running. My heart is racing. Not from the exertion, but from the panic that something happened while we were chasing down Jake's stalker. I'm more than convinced that's who that fucker is.

I beat Adrian to the door, but barely. The officer is standing in my living room talking to Bentley but turns towards us when we burst through the door.

"What's happening? Is everyone okay?" Adrian asks, eyes wide and panicking just as I am.

"Yes, sir," Bentley answers. "I called the police as soon as I got them to the bathroom. Jake was pretty freaked out. He said it was his stalker, so I didn't want him to be out here. And Raina said she recognized those eyes. She said it was her mom's lawyer boyfriend or whatever the fuck he is."

"I've never been so grateful to a seventeen-year-old for keeping my baby and boyfriend safe," I tell him, reaching out to shake his hand. "You have my respect and blessing."

"Thank you, sir."

The officer turns to me. "I'd like to talk to your daughter and boyfriend if possible."

"Can you just talk to us? We chased him. Got a good view of some tattoos," Adrian pleads. I know he doesn't want to retraumatize either of them.

"I need to verify things with them, too, sir."

Adrian sighs, but nods. I pull up my security footage as Bentley goes to get Raina and Jake. As they both give their statements, I look through the footage. As I suspected, there's no face. But we do get a clear view of him getting out of his car. And as he's walking past my front door, the camera catches his hand. As Adrian said, there's a spider tattoo on the top of his left hand. There's no clear view of his license plate, but I can definitely tell what kind of car he's driving. It's different from the one Adrian described that he ran off the road before. And different from what I saw when he took off after I got him away from Jake at the grocery store.

As soon as the cop is done talking to Jake, Raina, and Adrian, he turns to me to see if I have anything else to add. I show him the video and email it to the address he gives me. I don't know if this guy is in the system, but if he is, hopefully the tattoo description will help us catch him.

Because if he ever comes near my property or those I love ever again, I'll kill him with my bare hands and not blink an eye.

Chapter Thirteen

I jump a little at the knock on the door as my eyes blink open. I yawn. We all fell asleep on the couch last night watching a funny movie to get our minds off everything. *Ernest Scared Stupid*. I've never in my life heard of that movie, but Adam and Adrian both swore it was hilarious, and they came through. It was really funny. I didn't see the end, though, so we'll have to watch it again. I fell asleep long before that.

It was like the adrenaline just dropped from my body and took me down with it. I don't remember laying down, but I'm comfortable with my head on Adam's lap. Adrian is behind me with his arms wrapped tightly around me. His head is also in Adam's lap. Adam is sleeping sitting up with his long, powerful legs stretched out on the chaise of the couch.

Someone knocks again, and I groan. Adam stirs with a long sigh. "I'll get it," he mumbles.

Adrian and I lift our heads with simultaneous yawns as Adam carefully gets up. Adrian shifts slightly and moves his arm under my head so I can use it as a pillow. Still exhausted, I close my eyes with a content moan under my breath. Adrian kisses the back of my neck, sending chills down my spine and straight to my dick. Thankfully, I'm covered in a blanket.

"Hey, Caden," Adam says. That has mine and Aiden's head snapping up and looking towards the door.

"Hey. Can I come in? It's fucking wet out here."

"Yeah."

"I have some news for you. Don't know if it's going to be tough to hear or a damn blessing."

"I could use some good news. Shoes off if you need to talk to us all."

"You and Raina for sure."

We hear some chuckling and shuffling before Caden and Adam appear in the living room. We all sit up, Bentley and Raina included. Everyone looks as tired as I feel. Adrian arranges the blanket over us as Adam sits back down. Adam squeezes my knee as Adrian puts his arm around me and hugs me close. Raina yawns and rests her head on Bentley's shoulder as he wraps them both in a blanket.

Caden sits down in an oversized chair and leans forward, his elbows on his knees. "I don't know how y'all are gonna take this, but… uh… well, Carmen… she, uh… She's no longer with us." Caden eyes us all cautiously.

Adam narrows his eyes. "What… exactly are you getting at?"

Caden clears his throat. "She was found last night. I got a call to her place. It was a gruesome scene. I don't want to go into details around your daughter, man, but… she's gone. She's dead." Caden glances at Raina before looking back at Adam.

Adam gets up and walks to Raina. He kneels in front of her and takes her hands. She's staring straight ahead. Her lips are moving, but no words come out; no sound. Adam reaches up and tucks her hair behind her ear. Bentley hugs her even tighter. I want nothing more than to go to her and offer my own comfort, but I don't know if that's my place or not. I don't want to interfere or overstep any boundaries. I lean into Adrian unsure how to feel about this news and am comforted by the hug he gives me in return.

"Raina, say something, honey," Adam says.

"I don't feel sorry…" she whispers, her eyes wild. "Why don't I feel sorry?" Her voice is even lower. I barely catch the words.

"She put you through a lot. It's exhausting to feel empathy towards someone who doesn't feel it back. Someone who treated you like shit and abused you. It's okay. Your feelings, or lack thereof, are valid. It's nothing to feel ashamed about."

Raina nods as Bentley slowly gets up. "I think I should take you upstairs so they can talk. You might not feel like it matters much to you, but I don't want you to hear details right now. You can decide later if you want to hear them." He holds out his hand to her as Adam lets them go. Raina nods and takes Bentley's hand. He pulls her up and leads her up the stairs.

I'm liking this kid more and more. He's a take control kind of guy. Quick on his feet. Fast decision maker.

Once we hear Raina's door close, Adam stands and turns toward Caden. "Okay. Lay it on us."

Caden nods. "I was called last night. They needed a supervisor. It was gruesome. Very much cartel signs, only they were so obviously faked, it was almost comical, but there was one thing that threw me. It was so fucking personal. I couldn't get it out of my head."

"What was it?" I ask cautiously, not sure I really want to know.

"There was a picture of her with her attorney. They looked happy and in love. They were on a cruise. The back of the pic had words written on it. It said, 'Don't say a word. She's next. You can't stop me now'. It was nailed to her tongue, which had been cut out and hung on the wall."

Adrian gags under his breath. "Fuck me."

"There were other signs of trauma," Caden continues. "She was… violated… six ways to Sunday. She had a tire iron sticking out of her. She was cut over two-hundred times with a knife. Superficial wounds, but enough to cause her to suffer as she was bleeding out."

I look at Caden, horrified. It's my turn to gag. "Fuck me." I mimic Aiden's words because I don't know what else to say.

Adam stops pacing and looks Caden dead in the eyes. "I'm a suspect."

"Naturally, but I can clear you easily. Just need your surveillance and statements saying you've been here. You can email the footage from when you left to chase the intruder to when you got home until about five this morning. Do you have in house cameras?"

"A couple. Mostly in the common areas and hallways. Nothing in any private areas."

Caden nods. "Send it. Leave the footage from when you ran out chasing the intruder. I have other video footage from other people during that time. It tracks your movements. Her boyfriend attorney is already screaming at us to arrest you."

"Figures." Adam visibly rolls his eyes.

He's very calm, but my heart is in my throat. The thought of him being arrested upsets me beyond anything I've felt before. I can't bear the thought of being away from him now that I finally have him. The past couple weeks have been the best of my life. I can't lose that.

The entire day has been filled with silence. The most deafening silence imaginable. I never understood the saying about how silence can be so loud. How can something that's supposed to be the definition of quiet be loud? I understand now. There's tension in the air. Unspoken words hang like rain suspended in the atmosphere, waiting for enough precipitation to let loose and fall.

Raina stopped speaking all together. Bentley begged his parents and us to let him stay with her. They agreed after talking to Adam. Adrian spent the entire day keeping me sane. Caden assured us all before he left that Adam wouldn't be arrested, so I have no reason to be so worried. It probably has a lot to do with all of the events that happened in the past twenty-four hours. The court case. My stalker. Adam and Adrian chasing him. And then Carmen's brutal murder.

As I lay here staring at the ceiling, my mind won't stop. It keeps turning over the events in more and more detail until I find myself with a headache and inability to close my eyes.

Bump.

I sit straight up in bed, my eyes wide.

Beep, beep! Beep, beep! Beep, beep!

My head jerks to the beeping noise. Adam's phone.

"Mmm..." Adam groans as he turns towards his nightstand. He blindly grabs for his phone. "What are you doin' up?" he drawls in a sexy, sleep filled voice that would do things to me if I wasn't so fucking terrified.

Bump. Bump. Bump.

I grip Adam's leg as he looks at his phone.

"Did you hear that?" I whisper.

"Hear what?" Adam looks down at his phone.

Bump. Bump. Bump.

"That!" I whisper yell.

Adrian stirs next to me and rubs his hand over my lower back. "You okay?" he asks raspily. "Come lay back down."

Bump. Bump. Bump.

My heart is thumping, but I can tell that sound is getting closer.

"The fuck was that?" Adrian asks as he sits up in the bed.

Adam jerks into a sitting position. "Shit."

We're all sleeping naked, but the very second Adam starts pulling on jeans, Adrian and I are jumping out of bed and pulling on our own.

"What's going on?" Adrian asks quietly, but loud enough for Adam to hear.

"There's been a window breach," Adam whispers.

"Aaaah!"

We all freeze at the scream that cuts through the night air.

"Raina!" we all shout in unison as we run for the bedroom door.

"Adam!" Bentley screams out.

"We're coming!" Adam yells back. We all pound down the hall to Raina's bedroom. Adam reaches the door first and tries to open it, but it's locked. He wastes zero time in kicking it open with one swift boot to the door.

Raina is still screaming as someone attempts to drag her out the window. Bentley is trying to drag her back by her legs. Adam flies into the room at the very same time a leather gloved hand slaps tightly over my mouth. I flail and kick my feet out, hoping to hell they connect with Adrian's ass because he's running into the room behind Adam.

I shout into the glove and elbow my attacker as my toe hits Adrian with just enough force to get his attention. When he turns towards me, his eyes widen.

"Motherfucker! Let him the fuck go!" Adrian lunges towards my assailant.

"Come any fucking closer, I slit his throat," he growls just as I feel cold metal against my skin. I know that voice.

"Pope?" I question.

"Doesn't matter now, huh?" With his other hand, he rips off his mask. I hear a lot of commotion in the other room. I hope Adam and Bentley are getting Raina back. It's all I can think of. What's happening to me is nothing compared to if Adam loses his daughter. The knife sinks in a little more.

"Fuck me. You're Carmen's fucking attorney boyfriend," Adrian says, surprise swimming in the air. "Too bad, asshole." Adrian pulls a gun out from his waistband with a chuckle. My eyes widen in shocked relief. "Never bring a knife to a gunfight, Mr. Doyle. Let him go, or I shoot. And don't think for one second that I won't shoot your hostage. Can't leave here with him if he can't fucking move, can you?"

I might be young, but I know that line is from the movie *Speed* with Keanu Reeves and Sandra Bullock. Jeff Daniels used it after Keanu told him what he'd do in a hostage situation. Shoot the hostage always seemed like a smart answer to me. As long as the hostage isn't shot in any arteries and bleeds out. Cops are good shots. They can nick someone and make it look like there's a lot of blood.

I trust that Adrian is just as good of a shot. I've learned something about him and Adam over the last couple of weeks. They are never without a gun. And they are so well-versed in so many things, I am sure that gun use is one of their many talents.

"Not a chance, Mr. Sloan. I'm not stupid. I know you ain't shootin' your little boy toy."

"You really wanna try him?" I ask a little incredulously. Fuck. I wouldn't challenge him. Not with that look in his eyes.

I glance out of the corner of my eye and see Pope's arm is fucked beyond belief from his fight with the dogs last night. My guess is his face doesn't look much better.

"Alright! Alright! Look. We're backed up! Now, let her the fuck go! You're not getting out of here alive." Adam's voice sounds savage. I see Adam's and Bentley's shadows creeping into the hallway.

The distraction is just what I need to throw Doyle's arm off me and dive to the side. Aiden wastes no time. He shoots. The sound is deafening. I don't know if he shot twice, or if Adam took a shot at the other guy. All I know is my ears are echoing and ringing at the same time. I hear the audio around me go down comically. Like I'm in a movie. Aiden's lips are moving. I know he's asking if I'm okay, but I can't hear his voice.

I slump against the wall holding my ears and staring hard at Pope. Mr. Doyle. What the fuck ever. His face is all scratched. His left arm is bandaged up really well. His left is, too, but not as much. He really got his handed to him by those dogs.

Adam walks out of the room in slow motion hugging Raina close to him. He shields her face with his hand as Bentley moves his body in front of her to block her view of the chaos that's unfolded in the hallway.

I don't know where the other guy is, but the asshole who had a knife to my throat is currently holding his shoulder and whimpering about how he's going to die. While my hearing is slowly returning, the words coming out of his mouth sound demonic and psychotic. I can see each molecule of the blood dripping down his arm.

"Pope…" I mumble. The words leave my mouth the very second I think of them. With a roar, the world is suddenly righted.

"What?" Adrian asks, cupping my cheek. "Jake, talk to me. You okay?"

"Pope!" I say louder, pointing at Fucktard Doyle. "That's Pope!" I'm sure of it. I've never been more sure of anything else in my life.

"Shut up!" he bellows as he holds his wound. "Shut up! Shut up!"

"Jesus Christ," Adam growls. "It really is. I knew I knew that voice."

I look up as blue and red lights fill Raina's room and part of the hallway. "What happened to the other guy?"

"Dead," Bentley answers. "Dead."

His eyes are cold but burning with rage. Raina says nothing at all. She just curls herself even tighter into her dad. I don't think she's even crying. She's barely breathing.

Cops swarm the house. I see a familiar face in Caden and give him a tiny smile. He nods.

I don't know where we go from here, but I don't think anyone will want to stay at Adam's anymore. When the sense of security a person has is gone, it's never going to come back. I know this has brought us closer together, but Adam's house isn't safe anymore.

Not for Raina.

Not for me.

Not for anyone.

Chapter Fourteen

(Halloween)

"Ugh. Get me out of here. I'm sure we've seen this same skeleton before," Jake pouts.

I chuckle. "Just like we saw that same witch?"

"And ghost?" Adam chips in.

Jake nods. "Yes. To all of that. Did we get turned around?" He turns in an adorable circle, and I outright laugh.

I point towards Adam. "You know Adam has a map, right?"

Jake's mouth drops open. He turns to Adam with the saddest, betrayed expression on his handsome face. "You actually have a map? We could've used it this whole time?"

Adam's grin widens. "What the hell would the fun of that be?"

Jake's jaw drops. He blinks in mock disbelief. "That's it. I'm not talking to you anymore." He turns away, pouting as he crosses his arms. "You no love me no more."

Adam and I both look at each other and crack up. We both prowl to him. Adam picks him up with absolute ease and throws him over his shoulder. He swats one of his ass cheeks as I kiss the other. Jake lets out a surprised noise that can only be considered a squeak that has Adam and I laughing even harder as we take off running through the corn maze.

"Hey! Put me down, you fiend! You know I can walk!" Jake laughs as he swats Adam's ass. That causes nothing more than another swat to Jake's ass before Adam bites it.

I laugh. "You'll learn. One day. It'll be fun teaching you."

As soon as we reach the end of the maze, Adam finds the Spooky Hayride. Without setting down a laughing Jake, he speed walks straight towards it.

I follow, looking around. Walker Ranch is all decked out in Halloween decor. Everything is decorated in black and orange. There are skeletons, witches, ghosts, pumpkins, scarecrows, and even mummies and zombies. Frankenstein is driving the Spooky Hayride. There are black cat cutouts and witches brewing something in their big cauldron. They somehow have ghosts suspended in the air like they are flying above the ride and following us. Walker Ranch never half asses anything.

I fucking love it.

I can't wait for Christmas. Walker Ranch does things for every holiday, but Christmas is the most magical. They have a Wish Tree. I've always put the same thing each year. *For the one that I love to see me*. This year, my wish has come true and doubled. I have both Adam and Jake.

Adam sets Jake on his feet and guides him up the stairs onto the trailer. Jake grins and sits down. Adam grabs my hand, and those proverbial butterflies take flight. He leads me onto the trailer and sits me down on one side of Jake. He takes the other. Kids and parents load on, and we're all grinning like idiots. Like we're all kids again and enjoying all of this from that innocent child's perspective.

"Are you having fun?" I ask Jake.

"In all the years I've lived here, I've never gotten to come to Walker Ranch for anything. I've heard they have incredible events going on a lot. I asked to come here, but my parents always said no. I vowed to make it happen when I got kicked out, but I never got the chance. I was always busy working. Or too worn out to drag myself out of bed if I had the day off."

"Are you glad you got to come this year?" Adam asks.

"Yeah. Absolutely. Thank you both for bringing me along."

"Anytime, baby," I tell him as we both give his knee a squeeze.

"Haunted house next? Please say yes," Jake practically begs.

"I've been looking forward to it," Adam says. "Supposed to be the best one yet."

Seeing Jake's face light up is one of the greatest things I've ever seen, and it breaks my heart when it falls. "We're not getting to play the Halloween stuff in WOW, though. The Headless Horseman and the stuff you get was supposed to be pretty phenomenal."

I chuckle. "More important things in life than WOW. We're making our own adventure. And we've picked up some pretty good treats along the way." I smirk and wiggle my eyebrows.

We were alone for a bit in the maze and lost control. There was a lot of kissing and groping until we started hearing kids coming. When we pulled away, Jake was as red as a tomato. It was sexy as fuck to watch him come down as we continued on our way. It was even more pleasing to touch him and hear him suck in a breath.

The driver of the Spooky Hayride drops us all off at the haunted house. I pop up, pulling Jake with me. Adam laughs and follows us. We get in line for the haunted house.

"Dad!" Raina yells as she runs up to us and throws her arms around Adam. We're all dressed up as vampires. We agreed that we wanted family costumes, so we're a family of vampires.

"Hey, little one. Having fun?"

Raina giggles. "So much!"

"How was the haunted house?" Jake asks in anticipation.

Raina's eyes light up. "Oh my god, so much fun! You'll love it! We're going to get candy apples now!" Raina drags a laughing Bentley towards one of the vendors.

I can't help but laugh. "Looks like she's having fun."

"After everything she's been through, she deserves it," Adam laments.

He's not wrong. Jake's stalker really was Pope. Ric Doyle, in real life. He really was Carmen's boyfriend, doubling as her attorney. He was stalking Jake because he figured out who he was long ago. He wanted to teach him a real life lesson about what it's like to betray him, even though it wasn't betrayal at all, and it's just a fucking game. He didn't count on me and Adam also living here. Fate brought us to Jake. I won't even try to deny that. He was put in our lives at just the right time.

Pope's accomplice worked for the cartel. He was low ranking and wanted to work his way higher. He started a trafficking ring here in Piper Falls. The problem? He'd never done anything like that before. His first victim was meant to be Raina. He didn't count on Raina being such a smart girl. And he definitely didn't know that she has an entire Army behind her, starting with Adam, me, Jake, and Bentley.

It was Bentley that acted so quickly and saved Raina that night. Sure, Adam is the one who pulled the trigger, but Bentley is the one who fought that fucker and kept Raina in that bedroom. Had she been pulled out of the window, we may have never found her.

Adam's shot wasn't like mine. I shot to wound. Adam shot to kill. Pope's partner in crime died on Raina's floor. Pope himself ended his own life in prison. I asked Raina if it upset her that he wasn't going to face any justice for what he did. She told me, without blinking a fucking eye, that she prayed to Lucifer himself and knows Pope and his partner are being reserved a special place in hell. I've never been more proud.

Of course, with everything that happened in Adam's house, it started to feel unsafe. What happened was only a couple of weeks ago, but none of us have slept well. Raina wakes up screaming from night terrors even though she's moved to a different room. Jake has constant nightmares. Me and Adam just take turns sleeping because we don't ever want either Raina or Jake to feel unsafe in their own home.

And that's why we've decided we can build onto my home. We can add a pool and hot tub if we want to. We can add more to the garage. We can build onto the other side and add another room and bathroom. Even an office or library for Raina to study. I have plenty of room on my property to expand. We've started to move things over to my place. I thought Adam would be sad about leaving his beloved home, but he hasn't been at all. Jake and I have both talked to him, and his attitude is legitimately good riddance. He's ready to start over, with us, and we're all loving that.

I'm practically bouncing up and down by the time we go in. I've never told anyone, but haunted houses are my favorite part of Halloween. Talk about letting a person's kid out to play. That's what haunted houses are like for me. I love the costumes. I love the acting. I definitely love the scare.

But what I love most is being able to share the excitement with someone. While I have gone to haunted houses with people in the past, it's a lot different now that it's the people I love so much. It feels more wholesome; more joyful.

"Holy fuck!" Jake yells when we turn a corner and someone jumps out at him. He covers his mouth with both hands. "Shit! Fuck! Sorry! I can't swear with kids around!"

Adam cracks up as he puts his hand on Jake's back. He leans forward and kisses his neck as Jake leans into me, squeezing my hand tight. "Don't worry, sexy boy. We'll protect you." Adam grins. I can see Jake's cheeks turning red.

I give his hand a squeeze back as we continue. There are plenty more jump scares along the way. I love everyone's costumes, but my new favorite thing about haunted houses is Jake. It's like seeing them for the first time through his eyes. Everything is a wonder. Everything is new. The actors are phenomenal to him. It's like he forgets they're just people in costumes. I've been to so many that them being people in costumes is all I think about. I'm not immune to the wonder of it, I still love haunted houses, but I don't jump as much. I don't let myself lose control in the houses as often as I used to.

Judging from the pure fun on Adam's face, he agrees.

Once we reach the end of the haunted house, we're all smiling and laughing after genuinely having a good time. We meet Raina and Bentley by the caramel apples and get ourselves one. We decide to walk back to our car and take in all of the decorations along the way. The air is filled with happiness. It's hard not to be euphoric when being surrounded by this kind of vibe.

Once we're piled in Adam's truck and on our way back to my house, Raina starts laughing. We all glance at her.

"I was just thinking that everything that happened a couple weeks ago was like practice for Halloween." She grins devilishly, and all of us join in on the laughter to her dark sense of humor. Once again, that girl has made us all proud.

As soon as we reach the house, Bentley and Raina take off in his car. Adam and I arranged for her to stay the night with Bentley because we have our own plans. Until we soundproof our bedroom, we've been careful about our noise level when we do things together.

Not tonight.

Tonight is going to be some purely fucked up fun with the two men that I love.

"Go take a warm shower," I tell Jake once we get inside. "You deserve some pampering."

He gets a sexy look in his eyes. "Care to join me?"

I lean in and brush my lips against his. "More than you know. But I need you doing that so we can get the rest of your surprise for the night set up." I kiss him and swat his ass for good measure.

Adam grins and pulls him in for a kiss after I pull back. "You'll love it. Promise." He also swats Jake's ass as he gently pushes him towards the stairs and the shower in the master bedroom.

We stay downstairs locking up and turning out lights. Once we're sure the shower is running, we both walk up the stairs.

"You think he'll be up for this?" I ask, still a little bit unsure. "Fuck, I'm not even sure I'm up for it."

"He'll be up for it. And I promise you will be, too," Adam says confidently with a wink.

I grin. "Whatever you say."

"Damn right whatever I say."

I hold back the laugh because I don't want to alert Jake to our presence. I follow Adam into the room. He hands me a pair of my jeans and finds a tie. He goes to my drawer of fun stuff and pulls out leather cuffs for binding someone's hands and ankles.

"What are those for?"

"The cuffs are for Jake." Adam nods to the jeans in my hand. "Strip and put those on."

I do as I'm told as Adam pulls out two masks he hid in the closet. One of them is Ghostface from *Scream*. The other is from *The Punisher*. He tosses me the one from *The Punisher*. I grin as I catch it and put it on.

"When he comes out, we're both going to grab him," Adam says quietly as he strips, puts his jeans on, and then the mask. I have to admit he looks sexy as fuck. "We'll touch him a lot. The entire point is heightening his sense of fear and sense of sensuality at the same time. He'll realize it's us quickly, but his adrenaline will still be pumping. We'll take him to the bed. We'll secure his wrists to his ankles. And then we'll have our way with him while still allowing him control just like any other day. He can still tell us if it's too much. The same rules apply."

"Got it."

The shower turns off and we both quickly take our position on either side of the door so when he comes out, we can both grab him. I give Adam a smirk, though he can't see it behind my mask. I'm hoping Jake comes out naked. He has the perfect body to worship. Abs, muscles, a perky ass, and a dick I love having in my mouth and hands. It would be there all of the time if I had my way.

Jake opens the door and steps out. He's drying his hair with the towel, but as I wished, he's completely bare.

I wait for Adam to make his move. He steps behind Jake. I follow. He wraps one arm around Jake's neck from behind. I wrap mine around his waist. Jake sucks in a sharp breath. His eyes widen. He starts to fight until he sees the tattoo on Adam's arm.

Adam leans forward. "You know we respect you, right?" he growls, his voice low and buttery.

"Y-yes, sir," Jake breathes.

"Good. Because for the next few hours, it's going to look like we don't," I rumble in his ear, my already hard cock rubbing against him and begging for release.

"Oh fuck…" Jake's eyes roll back. He's already panting as Adam's hand moves down his body to his dick and mine moves to his ass.

I slap it as we move him towards the bed. His body jerks with a gasp. I watch Adam give his hardening length a squeeze. I moan and grab Jake's ass hard.

"Get up on the bed on your knees," Adam commands. Jake follows the order eagerly and without hesitation. Once he's in position, I watch

Adam cuff Jake's hands behind his back and secure them to his ankles like he's a fucking expert.

"Damn," I whisper.

Adam grins. "Just wait until it's your turn."

"Fuck me," I whisper again.

Adam crawls on the bed in front of Jake. He's watching us both like we're the air he pulls into his lungs. I crawl onto the other side of the bed in front of Jake and facing Adam. When Adam reaches out to touch Jake's body, I do the same. We start from Jake's head, face, jaw. We move down his collarbone, chest, arms, abs. I smirk as I watch him shiver at our touch.

He closes his eyes and lets his head fall back, but I'm not having that. I grip his jaw. "Open your eyes. Right now," I growl dominantly. I hear Adam's growl echo mine.

His eyes snap open like he's been burned. "Yes, sir."

I lightly tap his blushing cheek. "Good boy."

I allow one finger to trail down his throat, sternum, stomach, and stop at his base. His cock is rock hard and standing straight out for us. We both use one finger to tease it. We trace the veins on his throbbing dick. Precome is already beading at his tip. I swipe my finger through it and use it to slide my fingers easier over his cock.

The precome doesn't stop. Before long, he's dripping it. He keeps his eyes on us like a good boy, but we both know he's close to losing it. His thighs are trembling.

"Are you gonna come for us?" I ask, my eyes boring into his.

"Y-yes… please… please, sir… F-fuck… yes."

"Wait just a little bit, baby," Adam tells us both. He reaches for the button on his pants with one hand and undoes it like it's something he's practiced and perfected. He unzips himself and pulls out his dick never once stopping his slow torture of our sexy man.

I reach down to my jeans and do the same thing. I don't know if Adam practiced or not, but I definitely have. I reach in and pull out my cock. My eyes fall to both of my men. I'm a good size. Jake is definitely above average. We're all pretty thick, but Adam… fuck, he's huge. Definitely the kind of cock that makes me sing in ecstasy while he's rearranging my insides.

The thought has me smirking under my mask again, but that smirk quickly falls from my lips. I nearly choke when Adam reaches over and grabs my magic wand. He pulls it towards Jake and himself. Our swords all cross as Adam's large hand starts stroking himself while thrusting over Jake's cock and against mine. My breath hitches. So does Jake's.

"Ah… fuck… yes…" Adam moans. He locks his eyes on the three dicks as he strokes.

Shakily, since I'm damn close to coming, I grip my own cock. I start stroking and thrusting against him and Jake, following Adam's lead. I don't want to hit my release yet, but I fucking need Jake to.

"Come, my sexy little slut." My heart beats faster when Jake's dick thickens.

"Fuck!" Jake's thighs tremble. His eyes roll back in his head, and he comes. Explosively. "Fuck! Yes! Daddy!" Jake's entire body thrusts into the air between us as ropes and ropes of sticky, white goodness shoot from his pretty cock.

I raise an eyebrow behind my mask and look at Adam as we both slow down our own strokes. "Well, well. Someone has a hidden kink."

"This is gonna be fun," Adam says raspily. "Daddy, huh?"

"Oh, fuck." Jake pants as his body relaxes. Adam reaches around behind him and uncuffs him. I catch him as he collapses against me. I hold him close, rubbing his back.

Adam tosses the cuffs and stalks towards me holding a red, silk tie. I narrow my eyes when his hands reach towards my face. I know he's grinning under that mask as he lifts mine off. He says no words even when I look at him questioningly. He tosses my mask somewhere before gripping Jake and tossing him face first on the bed. He ties the blindfold around me. I don't have a chance to protest because Adam's lips are on mine in a hard and punishing kiss.

After taking my breath away, he grabs my hands and pulls me off the bed until I'm standing on the floor. "Stay right there for me."

I nod. I can't see a thing, but I can feel stuff. Like my pants being pulled to my knees; Jake being pulled to the edge of the bed.

"Like this?" I hear Jake ask.

"There we go. Just like that, baby," Adam says. "Good boy." I hear their lips meet and let out a low groan. I have no idea what's happening, but I trust Adam with my life. Whatever he's doing is bound to be enjoyable. He grips my hips. I feel his breath close to my lips. “Turn for me.” He guides me in the direction he wants.

I follow as submissively as I’ve ever been. An odd feeling for a man who doesn’t have a submissive bone in his body. I’d do anything he wants, though. Anything he asks. Anything he commands.

I stop when I feel him grip my hips tighter. “This where you want me?”

“Perfect. Don’t move.”

I don’t move a single millimeter. I can hear Jake let out a sexy groan. Adam chuckles and growls just enough to sound possessive.

“Fuck… that’s cold,” Jake says. My heart quickens.

“You’ll thank me for that in just a minute.” Adam grabs my cock a little roughly. I’m already harder than a diamond. I hiss at his touch and gasp out a moan when I feel cold lube on my length. Adam strokes it a bit before he lets go.

“Fuck…” I whisper. “What’d you let go for?” I give him a sexy half-smile.

“Oh, you’ll see.” Adam grips my hips once more and moves my body forward. I feel his hand on my hand as he guides it somewhere. I feel warm skin, but I don’t know who it belongs to.

I don’t know until I’m gripping a hard cock at the same moment that my dick falls against a tight little hole. It’s like magnets. I’m not trying to find his pucker, but the head of my hardened steel rod is, and it doesn’t take him long to find his target.

“Jesus, Jake. You’re so fucking hard, sunshine.” I give his dick a squeeze while gripping mine. Adam is behind me. Like Jake, lube is suddenly on my hole. I hiss at the cold of it, but moan because I know I’m about to get the ride of my life while also giving Jake the best of me.

“I really need you inside me,” Jake groans. “Now.”

“Patience, baby,” Adam says as he slams into me.

“Oh fuck!” I shout.

There’s no time to adjust to Adam. No time to tease Jake’s hole. Adam grips my hips and starts drilling my ass. The force and momentum of his thrusts cause me to slam into Jake just as hard. My hand automatically starts stroking him

"Ah!" Jake screams out. His dick immediately thickens. I stop stroking because I don't want him to come yet. Not without me and Adam. It's become a huge kink of mine to all reach our peaks together.

It's a good thing Raina isn't here because we're all moaning loud, shouting each other's names, and inventing new words of pleasure. The sounds of our skin slapping against each other, our dicks inside wet asses, and my hand beginning to stroke Jake once more… They are enough to drive me up the side of Crazy Mountain and careen into Ecstasy Ravine. I'm starved for them. Insatiable.

I push back into Adam with each thrust and pull Jake into me while I drive my dick deep into him. He clenches around me just as I am for Adam.

"Fuck, I'm close…" Adam rumbles in my ear.

"Me too!" I roar.

"Let me come!" Jake pleads. "Please, please let me come! I can't hold it!"

"Then you better cover my hand. Make a mess of me and this bed. Come on, sunshine. Show daddy what a good boy you are." I bite his neck. It's all it takes for him to clench his ass tight around me and shoot streams of sticky white cream all over the edge of the bed, the floor, specifically my foot, and my hand.

"Come, baby. Come with me. Now." Adam's teeth scrape my shoulder blades.

I hiss and throw my head back. I thrust hard and as deep as I can into Jake's ass. When I finally release my load, I'm howling like a fucking wolf. I grip Jake's hips hard, my arms shaking, as I fuck my come into him.

The same time I'm loading Jake's ass with me, Adam is filling mine. I feel like it's shooting right into my fucking stomach. We're all shouting each other's names. Come is spurting out of mine and Jake's ass. We're all trembling and panting as the last of our release flows out of us, making a far bigger mess.

After what seems like hours of laying over each other, our dicks sliding out of each other, Adam releases my blindfold. He pulls me up gently so I can see the actual mess we've all made of each other.

It's destruction...

It's chaos...

It’s beautiful…

Chapter Fifteen

(Thanksgiving)

“I still cannot believe Christmas decorations were up on November first,” Adrian remarks as he looks around the apartment.

“Raina and Jake took control. I had nothing to do with it.” I grin because secretly seeing the joy on their face was enough for me to agree to anything they wanted.

Adrian takes the turkey out of the oven. I agreed to let him cook it because I’ve had turkey cooked by him before, and it’s the best I’ve ever eaten. I don’t know what he does to it, but it’s a treat. I’ve even asked him, but he won’t tell me. He said it’s a secret he’ll take to his grave. But as long as he keeps making turkey until the day we all die, I’m okay not knowing what he does.

"Did you see the way Jake was grinning when he put Raina's Holiday Barbie on top of the tree as the topper?" I ask Adrian as he's checking the temp on the turkey.

He laughs. "Yeah. Raina was grinning from ear to ear. And Jake was all puffed out like he was doing the greatest thing in the world putting on that topper."

"I don't think Jake has ever had a real family holiday. There's so many things that we've already done that he's never done."

"I'm sure we'll figure it out the longer we're together and the more he opens up. But yeah. I'm with you. I think he's always been the black sheep even before he came out." Adrian puts the candied yams in the oven, and my mouth waters. Who knew sweet potatoes with brown sugar and marshmallows could taste so fucking good?

"You'd be right," Jake whispers from behind me. Adrian and I both turn towards him. He sits down on one of the high stools at the bar separating the kitchen from the living room. Adrian brings the potatoes to be mashed to the other side of the bar so we both can listen as he talks. We can tell he has something he wants us to know. Jake looks down at his hands and takes a breath. "They always knew something was wrong with me."

"First off, there's nothing wrong with you, baby," Adrian says. "Let's just get that straight."

Jake nods a little sadly. I put my hand on his thigh and squeeze to let him know he's not alone. "They said they always knew I wasn't like a normal boy. I played Barbie with my cousins. I liked fashion and dressing them up. And then we'd have a fashion show. My favorite Disney movie was *The Little Mermaid*. I wanted hair like Ariel's. I'd sing *Part of Your World* but change the words to, 'I wanna be where the mermaids are. I wanna see, wanna see 'em swimming'. For Halloween one year, I wanted to be Ariel. My parents made me go as King Triton instead. Whenever I sang the words to the song the way I wanted to, my parents corrected me into saying, 'I wanna be where the mermen are'."

"Jesus, honey." I rub his thigh soothingly.

"That's not even the worst part." His voice is barely above a whisper. I watch his shoulders rise and fall. Adrian has come around the counter and is sitting next to him doing the same thing I am. Jake still hasn't met either of our eyes, but that's okay. We're here anyway, and he knows that. "They sent me to a wilderness camp… It was…" He lets out a long breath as my red hot anger bubbles deep in the pit of my stomach. "It was bad. A step down from conversion therapy, but… barely… And… it was before I even came out to them. The camps aren't supposed to be longer than ninety days. At least that's what I thought. That's what they said when I first went. I was only ten. I was there for three years. I started cutting to keep the bad thoughts out. The ones they told me were bad. And that just kept up. I… I've been cutting longer than I led on…"

Adrian and I both just hug him. "It's okay, baby," I whisper against his neck. "They aren't bad thoughts. They are normal. Just because they don't agree doesn't mean they aren't normal. What's normal for them is what's in their little Bible bubble."

"You've turned out to be an incredible man, Jake. You're with two men who love the hell out of you. We're both happy to show you that you're incredible. There's nothing wrong with you. You're smart, handsome, talented. I don't know anyone who can whip up a coffee like you can while baking fucking delicious desserts." Adrian and I both grin when we see the corners of Jake's mouth twitch up as we pull away, still keeping our arms around him.

"I love you guys."

My heart skips a beat. I lean in and kiss Jake on the corner of his mouth. "Baby. I love you."

Adrian does exactly the same thing, only his cheeks are flushed. He lets one hand trail up to Jake's throat before he kisses the corner of his mouth. "I love you, Jake." He looks up at me and leans in to kiss me. "And I love you," he says just before our lips meet.

Once we pull away, I say, "I love you."

After a few more moments hugging, and maybe tearing up a little bit, Adrian goes back to the oven to pull out things I didn't even know he put in there. The green bean casserole that Raina made special for today. The candied yams. The broccoli cheese casserole I made. The turkey is stuffed with cornbread stuffing. He puts the rolls in the oven as Jake and I get up to help put everything out.

I call for Raina as we set the table. Jake heads to the kitchen to grab the other dishes Adrian is creating. Jake baked a pecan pie and pumpkin cream cheese pie yesterday. Adrian is putting in the apple pie Jake made. He sets a timer for it.

“There. All done. Food is all set up.” Adrian washes his hands before grabbing a carving knife and fork. He brings them over and hands them to me.

I blink before slowly taking them. “You… this…” I clear my throat. “You always carve the turkey,” I say, my voice low. “It’s your house.”

“It’s our home,” Adrian tells me, his voice just as low. “And as the dominant in this relationship and in our lives, the honor of turkey carving is passed on to you.” He pulls out the chair at the head of the table for me. Jake sits to my right. Raina sits to my left. Adrian takes his seat across from me.

I let out a breath and turn towards the turkey. “Man, we’ve been through a lot this year,” I begin as I look at each one of them. “Yet somehow, we’ve managed to end up here with each other. It’s been a long road. I feel like I’ve lived several lifetimes these past few months. But we’re finally all where we belong. That’s what I’m most grateful about this year.”

“Can I get a hell yeah?” Adrian says with a grin as he raises his champagne glass filled with sweet tea.

“Hell yeah!” we all say in unison. We clink glasses.

I start cutting the turkey with the biggest smile on my face than I think I’ve ever had.

This is our first Thanksgiving as a family.

Our new beginning…

I come out of the bathroom to a sight that has my dick rock solid. Adrian has Jake pinned to the bed. I watch as he kisses his way down Jake’s abs. Jake’s moans are addictive and have my feet walking towards the scene of their own volition.

I slide my hand over Adrian’s ass. “Starting without me, I see.” I grin when he looks back at me and slap his ass.

He sucks Jake’s cock into his mouth as I’m climbing on the bed. I give myself a few pumps as I straddle Jake’s chest. Jake opens his mouth eagerly with a sexy as fuck smile. He lets his tongue roll out like it’s a red carpet welcoming me. I slap his tongue with my cock before slowly sliding it in. I groan as the wet heat of his mouth envelops my dick.

"Mmm," Jake moans around me, and I groan again as the vibrations shoot straight down my spine.

I glance behind me and smirk as I watch Adrian tease Jake's tip with kitten licks and small sucks. Jake's hips automatically try to arch up, but Adrian holds them down as he takes Jake's length into his mouth. Slowly. Inch by inch.

It's driving Jake crazy. He's desperately sucking on me like he's trying to get Adrian to follow his lead. His tongue is swirling rapidly around my cock. I grin down at him and start thrusting slowly into his mouth. Once I touch the back of his throat, his eyes go wide, and he gags.

I pull back slightly to help him. I watch him slowly relax as he's able to take in air. Once he's calm, I tap his cheek lightly, and slide my dick to the back of his throat once more. I groan as he allows me deeper into his throat. "That's my good boy." I stroke his throat with my fingers before pulling back again to allow him to breathe.

I reach behind me, tangling my fingers in Adrian's hair and tugging lightly. Adrian moans around Jake, looking up at me with sultry eyes. Jake's resulting moan sends a shiver down my spine as my dick starts to thicken.

Not wanting to come yet, I pull out of his mouth and lean down, kissing Jake deeply. I nip his lip as I pull back and move off of Jake's chest to his side. I tug Adrian's hair, pulling him up off of Jake's dick with a quiet 'pop'.

"Fuck…," Jake whimpers, cheeks flushed with arousal.

I smirk and tug Adrian's lips to me, kissing him deeply, groaning at the taste of Jake's precome on his tongue.

"Mmm… Adam," Adrian moans, sucking on my tongue. I pull back, nipping his tongue with a possessive rumble.

A rumble from deep within my chest breaks free as I'm looking at Adrian then down at Jake. I maneuver Adrian until he's straddling Jake's hips. I give his ass a spank as I move between Jake's thighs. I shift his legs so his thighs are braced on mine, my dick nudging his hole, causing Jake's dick to nudge against Adrian's.

I grip Adrian's hips and push him down on Jake's cock as I thrust into Jake. Everyone shouts out a moan of pleasure. Jake's thighs tremble as he gets used to my size. Adrian leans back, arching slightly as he gets used to Jake.

I don't want to wait, I'm already seated deeply. And with a newly soundproofed room, I don't need to worry about anyone being quiet. So, when I give Jake a hard thrust, I grin widely as he screams.

"Ah! Adam!"

Jake's dick slams deeper into Adrian. "Fuck yes," Adrian groans. He uses Jake's thighs to brace himself as he starts bouncing up and down, slamming himself onto Jake's throbbing length.

Jake is so tight around me. He feels so good. He grips me as hard as he's gripping the sheets right now. He knows he has no control. His pleasure is in mine and Adrian's hands. He pulses around me. My thrusts move him up into Adrian, who is still bouncing on him hard and fast. I'm matching his pace. Jake's pleasure is rising higher and higher. I can see his balls tightening.

"I can't take anymore," he growls as he reaches for Adrian's cock and starts stroking at the same rhythm he's getting fucked.

I look over Adrian's shoulder just so I can watch. One of my new favorite things is the look on Adrian's face when he's getting fucked while his dick is getting stroked.

Or sucked.

It's like his ecstacy is so high that all he can do is form an 'O' with his mouth. No sound comes out except panting and moans. His eyes roll back when my lips touch his neck. He's trembling as much as Jake is. I know neither of them are going to last long.

I give Jake a few more hard thrusts before reaching around Adrian and playing with his balls while Jake strokes him.

"Oh… holy… ah!" Adrian moans. He's thick and ready. Jake is writhing under him and squeezing me tighter with each thrust.

I'm close, but I'm not there yet. I thrust faster… deeper… harder.

"Fuck, Adam… Please! Please!" Jake begs.

"I'm gonna… I…" Adrian manages to spit out.

"Come," I command.

It's all they need. Jake goes rigid. The only movement is the thrusts I'm giving him that force his dick into Adrian's pretty little ass. He comes so hard that it almost instantly starts gushing out of Adrian. The sound that comes out of his mouth as he convulses with the sheer release of his orgasm is a cross between a scream, a moan, and something far more primal.

"Ah!" Adrian screams out. Ropes of sticky, warm goodness shoot out of him with a force great enough to hit Jake's face and chest. As the orgasm subsides, the come travels to Jake's stomach. The sight is so fucking sexy, that when my orgasm hits, I'm completely shocked I'm not shooting Adrian to the ceiling.

"Yes!" I roar as a jet load of myself fills Jake's ass. Jake moans, taking everything I give him as his sexy dick spurts all that's left onto Adrian.

Jake is panting. His body has fallen limp as he breathes hard. I wrap a hand around Adrian's throat and turn him to me so I can kiss him with all my soul as my cock finishes inside Jake. Once I release him, he leans over and kisses Jake with the same amount of passion and ferocity as I gave him. When he pulls back, his chest is just as covered in his own come as Jake's is.

I pull out, slowly, reveling in the squelching noise Jake's ass gives me as it's releasing me from its grip. Adrian is still straddling Jake. Jake's dick is still deep in Adrian. Once the two of them part, I crawl to Jake's side and lean in. I kiss him deeply, licking Adrian's come off his lips.

I love the noises he and Adrian make when I kiss them. As I get up, it's like they're both speaking in the sexiest satisfied moans, I've ever heard. I head for the bathroom to clean up. When I'm done. I grab a couple wet cloths and towels. I walk back to the bedroom to see them laying side by side with their eyes closed. They're holding hands and have the softest of smiles on their face. Their cocks have gone soft, but are still big and flopped over on their base.

I kneel next to Adrian and clean him up, towel drying him after. I'm pretty sure he's falling asleep, if he's not asleep already, because the noises he's making are the same ones he makes when he's having a good dream.

I lean over him and start cleaning up Jake. Once I finish, I towel him dry. I walk back to the bathroom to hang the clothes and towel up. I don't like putting wet cloths in the laundry basket. They start to smell like mildew. I don't like it.

After I'm done, I head back to the bedroom and see that Adrian has moved to his side. He and Jake have gotten under the covers. Jake's back is to Adrian. The blankets are open on my side so I can easily crawl in.

"Open the window a bit, baby," Adrian rumbles. "It's fucking hot."

I laugh. "The air is at like seventy-two"

"Dying," Jake says. "But blankets are comfy."

I grin and shake my head. I crack the window open for them and shut off the light. I crawl into bed with them, wrapping myself in the blanket. Almost instantly, I know how they're feeling. "Okay, the window was a good idea. The night is cool."

"Told you," Adrian mumbles.

I wrap my arms around them both. As we all lay naked and content, we drift off into a peaceful dreamland unaware that Jake's entire world is about to shatter…

Chapter Sixteen

(Two Weeks Later)

"Jake, get out of here, or you're not gonna make that funeral," Jo, the owner of the store, says as she bustles in. She's an older grandmotherly woman who has owned this shop for a long time. I love her to death. She has a sharp wit, even though she's the nicest person anyone will ever meet. "I appreciate you holdin' down the fort for me, but you gotta go."

I nod, the slightly happy mood shifting suddenly. "Yeah. Thanks, Jo." My heart feels like it's breaking. No. Not breaking. It feels like it's been ripped out of my chest and stomped on, and then shoved into a blender.

Henry.

He was like a grandfather to me. Nicest guy. Everyone in town liked him. He's been sick for a while, and the sicker he got, the more time I spent around him. I just helped him with his lawn. Just played cards with him. I just bought him groceries and that chicken he liked so much. Just made sure he was stocked up on his favorite sweet tea. He looked worse for the wear, but I hoped everything would be okay.

Now, he's gone. I knew it was coming, deep down, but it's still hard. I'd grown really close to him over the past few months. There's no way I'll miss this funeral. I don't care where I am or what I'm doing. I'd drop it all just to say my last goodbyes to one of the greatest men I've ever known.

And so close after Thanksgiving…

I hurry to the bathroom and quickly change into the black suit pants and a black shirt I brought with me. I forego the jacket because Texas is scalding hot, even though we're well into December.

Once I'm presentable, I quickly say goodbye to everyone working on my way out to my Adam's truck. He's been allowing me to use it since I no longer have one.

The second I start it, I'm blasted with hot air. I don't have time to let it cool down, so I sigh and back out of my spot, prepared for the first few minutes to be sweltering. I put the window down until the cool air starts. Once I hit the freeway, I'm lost in thought.

The way Henry smiled was infectious. The way he laughed always brought a smile to my face no matter how dark the day was. His approval of Adrian and Adam meant the entire world to me when I brought them to introduce to him. I didn't realize I needed that until he did it. He brightened my heart. Knowing my happiness was important to him in his last few days keeps me going.

Especially since his smile could've lit the room on fire. It was so brilliant and illuminating. I believe it brought him peace knowing I'll be okay. Taken care of and happy. He never said it, but I know he could see how hard things have been for me. I know he knows I wasn't happy, no matter how hard I tried to fake it. He saw the difference when Adam and Adrian came into my life. He was a silent supporter.

Henry…

I'm really going to miss you, man.

The funeral was as dreary as it possibly could've been. I sat with Adrian and Adam. Adam kept his arm around me. Adrian was squeezing and rubbing my thigh. I'm so grateful that they were there for me. I don't think I could've gotten through everything without them. I broke down more times than I can count. The next time was no better than the time before. I don't know how I managed to stay quiet while blubbering like a complete idiot.

Adam sits next to me and hands me a glass of iced water. "Here, baby."

I shake my head. "I'm not thirsty," I whisper.

"You also lost a lot of hydration while you were crying. Please drink the water. You can cry all you want, and we'll hug you through it all, but I don't want you dehydrated." There's such a tender tone to his words that I'm reaching for the water just to please him. I sip it because I know better. Gulping helps no one, especially me.

Once I take a few sips, I start to set the glass on the table. Adam takes it from me instead. I lean back on the couch watching Adrian move around the kitchen.

"I know I haven't eaten much, but… I don't think I can…"

"You can eat a few bites off my plate, if you want, but I'm not going to let you not nourish your body." Adam keeps the water in his hand as he leans back. He puts his arm around me and hugs me close to him. "I don't know what he's making, but it'll be something easy on you and your stomach. I know you're not feeling the best either."

"Nervous stomach," I say as I hug myself while snuggling as close as possible into him.

"Raina! Dinner!" Adrian calls up the stairs. He brings over a bowl of something with some crackers. "There's not a lot in this bowl, but it's homemade chicken noodle soup. I started it this morning. Just finished it up. I need you to eat what you can here. I don't want you stuck in your head and not getting any kind of nourishment." He hands me the bowl.

I take it with a low chuckle. "I'm not making promises."

"Baby, a bite of it will make us happy. It means you're trying," Adam tells me as Adrian leans down to kiss my forehead. He hands Adam his bowl and puts crackers on the table for us before heading back to the kitchen.

Adrian dishes up himself and Raina as she bounds happily into the kitchen. I know she didn't just attend the funeral of someone, but she could stand to be less chipper while I'm going through hell.

She didn't attend her mother's funeral. She chose to stay far, far away. No one could find any fault in that decision. Later on, she had a little bit of a breakdown because she didn't know how anyone could treat their daughter like her mother did to her. She screamed. She cried. We all sat around and hugged her until she felt stable enough to let go.

I'm trying to fight my own breakdown. Henry was such a good person. He was always around when I needed an ear, even in the last few days of his life. He brought joy to me. I made sure to tell him that over and over. He just said to keep following my heart no matter what life throws at me. Very much Henry.

"How can such a good person be taken away like that? I feel like he had many more good years." My hands are freezing cold. I feel dizzy and sick. I put my soup down because my hands are shaking. My heart starts beating faster. I stand up and immediately head for the stairs.

Maybe it's my turn for a breakdown.

The second I reach our bedroom, I close the door and let out a blood curdling scream as I drop to my knees. There's suddenly black spots impeding my vision, but they are secondary to the fact that my head and lungs feel like they're going to explode.

I let out another scream. The tears burst like a damn from my eyes. Gut wrenching screams and sobs explode from my throat. I feel arms around me, but it does nothing to calm the storm brewing within. It's like a hurricane. Category six. It doesn't exist to the weather people, but it's what's happening to me right this moment. Rain is lashing. Wind is howling. Waves are crashing. Tornadoes are destroying.

"Why!" I scream. "Why does this so-called god take good people away, but all the bad people get to stay? What kind of god strikes down innocent people, but lets pedophiles, murderers, and other terrible people live?"

"There's no answer, baby…" Adam whispers in my ear. "There's no answer…"

I cry for a long time while Adam and Adrian hug me. Raina is rubbing my back. Sometimes, I feel her cheek against it. My heart feels like with each tear, a piece of it is floating away. The loss is the most earth shattering thing I've ever experienced.

"He was my only family for a long time. I'm close to the owner of the coffee shop, but Henry… he was like the uncle, or even grandfather, that I always wanted but never had. Losing him was like… it's like losing a part of myself. The only part that was good."

"You have more good in you than you think," Adrian whispers in my ear.

"And more good in your life," Raina says as she hugs my back, rubbing it gently. "I'm glad we've met you and have you in our life."

I don't know what comes over me, but I turn to her. A fresh wave of tears overflows as I hug her as hard as I dare. Hearing the words from Adrian and Adam is comforting. Beautiful. But knowing that Raina accepts me, that she thinks I'm good… that somehow means everything.

Raina…

Adrian…

Adam…

These people, this family, is my entire world. I know that no matter how much my world crashes around me, no matter how hard I fall, they will always be here for me. They'll always protect me and keep me safe.

And they'll be the hands that keep me from slipping away…

Chapter Seventeen

(One Week Later)

"Oh my god, I'm so excited. This is one of my favorite Christmas events," Jake says with a huge grin. "I can't wait for you guys to see our storefront display."

Every year, there are events the week before Christmas. They always start on December twelfth and end December eighteenth. We start with the Christmas tree lighting ceremony. After that, the storefronts in town reveal their decorated storefronts. All the stores try to go all out and build huge Christmas scenes.

There have been a lot of winners. Last year, a storefront won with a manger scene. Except it wasn't the typical Jesus, Joseph, and Mary scene. It was them in a sense, but they were played by Barbie and Ken. The Barbie dream house was behind them. The donkey was Barbie's horse. I absolutely hated it, but the rest of the town thought it was the best scene. They got a ton of votes.

It surprised me because it seemed almost blasphemous in the Bible Belt. Jesus wasn't about money and flashy things. He was about everything exactly the opposite of that. In fact, he was basically against it completely. I felt like that storefront missed the mark so badly that they were in a whole other world.

Jake told us it also helped everyone at Cozy Bean decide what they needed to do. They'd always decorated more on the subtle side, but people seemed to really like flashy and in their face. So this year, they went all out. He won't tell us what they did, but he's been bouncing about it all day long. They put up the finishing touches this morning.

"We can't wait to see what Cozy did," I say, hugging him and kissing him on the head.

"I'm sure it'll be great," Adam remarks with a grin.

"Ladies and Gentleman!" the Mayor of Piper Falls begins. "Thank you for coming to the kickoff of the town's events. We hope you'll stick around to enjoy the hard work our storefronts here in downtown have put in creating their beautiful Christmas window displays. I'm looking forward to seeing them all, and I hope you are, too! Don't forget about our Gingerbread House contest tomorrow. We have our Christmas cookie contest Wednesday. Thursday is our Christmas ornament decorating contest. Friday is the annual parade. Santa did inform me that he will definitely be here with all eight of his reindeer and even a couple of elves! Saturday is our ice sculpting contest sponsored by our Sportsbike Club. You'll see me there competing! And we conclude Sunday with the Wish Tree up at Walker Ranch. All families who need a Christmas meal to cook Christmas day will not leave without one. With all of that said, give me a countdown! Ten!"

"Nine!" everyone in the crowd says in unison. "Eight! Seven! Six!"

Jake and Adam wrap an arm around me.

"Five! Four! Three! Two! One!"

The Mayor hits a big button, and the lights on the tree brilliantly shine. We all clap and cheer. I look down the street and see all of the storefronts pulling down curtains to reveal their decorations. I'm excited to see what Jake and everyone has done at the Cozy Bean.

"Come on! I want you to see what we've done at work!" Jake excitedly takes both mine and Adam's hands and pulls us towards the Cozy Bean.

I laugh. "Someone's excited!"

"I have been waiting weeks to show you this. I wanted to tell you guys our idea, but we swore everyone to secrecy. Also, I wanted you to be surprised!"

Adam grins as we follow Jake. He's charging through the crowd like it's something he does everyday. The closer we get, the more Jake picks up speed. We're practically running by the time we get to it. He stops in front of it and looks at us with wide, twinkling eyes and a huge grin.

"Holy shit," Adam says as he takes it all in.

I smile. They have an entire town set up complete with an iced over pond in the middle. There are small, carved, wooden people all dressed in winter clothing skating around the frozen pond. They're actually moving. They have people walking in the town. Some are facing each other talking. Their arms and heads move.

But my favorite part is the steam train that comes through. It chugs through the town and disappears in a tunnel. Peering into the cafe, the train can be seen chugging through the entire store. Up and down hills, through other tunnels, passing near tables before it ends up back in the little town tooting its horn. There's snow on the ground that looks as sparkly as a first snow blanketing the world in it's quiet beauty.

Even the window has pristine detail. It's frosted. It looks like snow is falling gently and quietly. With the lights from the street and from the cafe, when I move, it looks like the snow is also moving as it catches the light. It's like I'm standing on a mountain top peering down at a little Christmas town.

"It's fucking perfect," I nearly whisper, my eyes taking in every single picture perfect feature. Even the inside is decorated to look like customers are outside in a winter wonderland. There's no element not captured.

Jake is grinning and bouncing on his toes. "Do you like it?"

"Baby, it's amazing. There's no words to describe how breathtaking this is," Adam says, his eyes focused on the scene in front of him. "It's just..."

"Stunning," I finish when Adam loses the ability to speak. "It's like I'm a kid again seeing winter and Christmas for the first time."

"Yes! That was absolutely the goal." Jake fist pumps the air.

I take the voting cards out for the three of us and hand each of them the card. "I don't think we need to discuss the winner. It's Cozy Bean for sure."

"I hope they win," Adam remarks. "Fuck, I don't think I've ever seen Cozy Bean win. It'd be cool walking in and seeing their plaque hung up proudly saying they won."

"I'm excited for the big trophy we get to parade around on the float we have for Friday's parade."

I hug Jake. "I'm so proud of you. I know you're gonna get that trophy. Can't wait to see it on your float."

Adam takes his turn to hug Jake before all walk hand in hand along the street looking at all of the storefronts as we pass. "No other storefront compares, in my opinion." Adam turns in a partial circle. "The rest of these are just bland and boring. I know they took effort. You can see the heart in them, but man. They just don't compare to Cozy Bean. Such a classic and beautiful scene."

"Couldn't agree more," I say.

But it's the absolute pure joy on Jake's face that really does it for me. He's so proud of his work and the work of his team that it just radiates off him.

He's glowing, and it's fucking perfect.

❄❄❄

Adam and I stand with Raina and Bentley. His parents, little sister, and little brother are with us. We're in the midst of the parade. Cozy Bean did win the storefront contest. Their float is the one just before Santa. We're so beyond proud of him. He's been on a high ever since the storefront winners were announced. He and his coworkers worked hard on that display. They deserved the win and all of the accolades they're about to have.

"This week has been a whirlwind. I don't think I've ever gone to every single Christmas event." Adam grins as he looks at me. "It was fun."

"It was fun seeing it all through Raina's and Jake's eyes, that's for sure."

"That Gingerbread House contest? Hands down my favorite."

"Not the storefront reveal?" I tease.

Adam laughs. "Funny. I meant after that. Mila West I think her name was. Just a nice plain looking house with lots of animals. I don't have a clue how they did those horses, but that was amazing."

"The cookie contest was fun. I'm glad Bluebonnet Bakery won."

"They deserved it. Margaret would've been proud. Man, I miss her. She made the best coffee vanilla cookies."

"Evie stuck to that recipe. I'm glad because those things are to die for."

"What about those Christmas ornaments, though?"

"They were good. The winners did amazing, but I still think Raina's blew them all out of the water. She put a lot of heart into hers." I smile as I remember the joy on her face making it.

"At least we get to hang it on the tree."

"Front and center."

"I wouldn't allow anything else." Adam grins. "I'm really looking forward to tomorrow."

I smile and squeeze his hand, leaning into him a little. "You look forward to it every year. Ice sculpting is one of your favorite things to do. And you're the one who came up with the idea of adding it into the annual events."

"It's my baby."

"Here he comes!" Bentley's little brother shouts. "Daddy! Daddy! Up! Up!"

"Come here, munchkin." Bentley's dad lifts up the boy. His little sister looks up at Bentley and just holds up her arms without saying anything after she sees her brother on her dad's shoulders.

Bentley wastes no time picking her up and putting her over his shoulders just like his dad did with his brother. "Up you go, little bear!"

She squeals and holds on tight to Bentley's head until she sees Jake. Then her little arms start waving around. "Jakey! Jakey! Jakey!" She grabs for him, and Adam and I both burst out laughing. We've all become close with Raina's boyfriend's family over the past few weeks, but I think the little kids have decided Jake is their big brother, too.

Jake jumps off the float and jogs to us. He gives Adam and I a quick kiss before dropping a load of candy in the little girl, Madison's, open candy bag. He does the same for the little boy, Holden.

"Love you guys!" Jake takes off at a jog to catch up to his float while he tosses candy out for the other eager kids.

"That float turned out better than I imagined," I say.

"Holy fuck, yes," Adam agrees.

The float is a replica of their window display, but they built a platform at the back of the float that displays a giant, three foot trophy that says 'Best Storefront Christmas Display' on it. The store that wins the contest each year gets to hold the trophy for one year before they need to pass it along to the next winner. Unless they win for years in a row, like Bluebonnet Bakery did. They won for something around five years before being dethroned by Papi's. I can't remember who held it last year, but before that, we had a nice battle going between the Golden Fleece and Unique Boutique. The competition is the best part sometimes.

This year, though, it wasn't the competition at all. It was how happy Jake was to present it to us, and the incredible way it brought us all back to our childhood.

Back when everything was innocent.

Something everyone needed after so much chaos.

A sweet calm…

Something only Christmas can bring.

Chapter Eighteen

❄ Adam ❄

"Ready for this?" Brax asks as we gather at Papi's. We have everything set up for the ice sculpting contest. Everyone is wearing coats and gloves to stay warm since we have specialized equipment set up to keep the ice from melting.

Adrian grins and rubs his hands together. "I was born ready. My partner is all psyched up and ready to go. Did you know she's only fifteen? Talented beyond belief. She's a painter. Name is Lara."

I nod. "I have a seventeen-year-old named Brandon. He just started riding. Got himself a two-hundred. Handles it well. Kid is impressive."

"I've ridden with him a couple of times," Brax chimes in. "He's got raw talent on that bike. I have Emily. She's thirteen and really wants to ride." He grins when he spots her. "There she is! First one here must mean good luck for me."

Adrian and I laugh. "Yeah, so you think. I'm taking that crown this year," Adrian challenges as my teammate comes in. "And there's my girl now! Lara! Over here!" Adrian waves.

I roll my eyes and go back to prepping our area. Everyone's partner shows up one by one. Teens and parents come in. Jason Andrews, the owner of Papi's, hands out gift cards to the teens who show up. That's part of what we do. We want to make sure that teens also have a good Christmas. A lot of stuff is geared towards kids. Teens often get left out. We make sure that's not the case with us.

"Hi," a shy young woman says to me, waving shyly from below the stage we've built for the competition.

"Hey. What's up?" I ask looking down at her.

"I… just um… I'm sixteen now, and… well, I thought… um…" She clears her throat, and I smile as I kneel down so I'm closer to her and can hear better. She plays with her fingers and looks down. "I… wanted… to ride… but… my parents… They won't let me?"

"Awe. I see. Well, here's some advice. Pick out a bike. Do your research. You can always get a hold of me by calling the number on the brochure we have out at the table by the door. I'm the president of the club. We have lots of people who can help you research. We have lots of meets. You can come by and talk to us. Look at our bikes. Save up as much as you can to get your license and your bike. They can't stop you when you turn eighteen right?"

She looks up at me, and I wink. She grins. "Right."

"Don't be afraid to reach out. Keep in touch with us. Follow us on all of social media. We're everywhere. We say where we're going to be and everything. Contact info is there. You can message us. You can ask to speak to a certain person if you'd like to. We're happy to talk. And we can help you learn how to ride."

She nods again with a bright smile. "Thank you so much! That means a lot to me. Um… you're…?"

I reach out my hand to shake hers. "Adam."

"Adam." She shakes my hand. "I'm Jessica."

"Nice to meet you, Jessica. Go grab our brochure. There's free merch there, too. Then hang out and watch the contest. I'm planning on winning." I flash her another grin as I stand. She giggles and runs off just as I catch a glimpse of my partner. He hurries to the stage with his head down.

"Sorry I'm late," he mumbles as rushes up the stairs.

"No worries. I've got everything set up. We have our design. You okay?"

"Just my dad. He's kind of a dick. Doesn't like that he can't control where I want to go to college. Hates I was already accepted at his rival university."

I nod. "Understood. But it's your life. Not his."

He smiles. "I know. I don't think he'll be here, though. If I win that grant money, can you keep it until I turn eighteen? I wouldn't put it past him to keep it."

I raise an eyebrow. "Shit, really? Yeah. Yeah, of course we'll keep it."

Little does he know that even if he doesn't win, he's getting that grant. From what I've learned about him, he's had a rough life. He could use a break. Damned if I'm not going to give him one.

"I could definitely use a job until I graduate. Don't know if you know anyone hiring. Maybe put in a good word for me. I've applied places, but when I roll up on my bike, it's like I suddenly have the plague."

"Oh, I know how that goes. Bikers have a terrible rap. We're bad boys who cause trouble and don't care about nothin' or no one."

"Hit that nail on the head." Brandon looks at all the tools. "So, what's first?"

"First, I'll be using a chainsaw to carve out our outline of our angel. From there, we'll chisel and carve the rest of her. I'll help you along. Guide you. It's all about teamwork. Even if we don't have the greatest looking angel, the point is that we tried our best as a team."

"I'm all in." Brandon looks up at the clock and sees we have a couple minutes as Jason starts talking.

"Good afternoon everyone. Welcome our contestants to the annual ice sculpting contest sponsored by our local Sportsbike Club!" There's immense applause as we all wave while people take their seats. Raina, Bentley, and Jake are all front and center. "Our contestants today are all teens from our great town and members of the Sportsbike Club. Every contestant here will be receiving a five-hundred dollar gift card!" More thunderous applause and cheers from the participants. "And our first place winner will receive a ten thousand dollar scholarship to any college they choose! Good luck. Contestants, get your chainsaws ready. We start in five!"

The crowd starts counting down with Jason. "Four! Three! Two! One!"

"Go!" Jason shouts.

There's a loud roar as we all start our chainsaws. Ice flies everywhere, including into the audience. Some laugh. Some squeal. I'm laser focused on each cut. Too much will ruin everything. Too deep too quickly can cause a fracture in the ice. It could collapse into pieces on us. We've got backups, but having to start over sucks when there's a time limit. We only have two hours.

After getting the initial outline cut, I gesture Brandon over. I show him how to chip away particular pieces to define our shape even more profoundly. The kid is a natural, and I'm very proud of him. I only have to give him directions one time before he's doing it on his own.

"Ooh… They're doing a dolphin, I think!" Raina shouts. I furrow my brows and glance at Brandon. He's looking at the sculpture next to us.

"That's Adrian and Lara!" Jake comments, surprised.

I turn and see they have an adult and baby jumping out of the water, but they have a long way to go to finish.

"Don't pay attention to anyone but us," I say to Brandon.

He shakes his head and gets back to work. "Thiers is coming out really well."

"Yeah, but ours is coming along just as well. It's anyone's game. We need to focus on us and our strategy."

"Yes, sir."

"You said you wanted a job. Want to work on my crew? I'll give you some work for the year until you leave. After that, you've got a summer position until you graduate." It's something I've been thinking about ever since he mentioned it. With only forty-five minutes left in the contest, I feel like he needs an extra boost.

"Hell yes. Absolutely. I'd love that, sir."

"You got it. We'll work out the details after the holidays. How's that sound?"

"Perfect. Thank you!"

We work tirelessly as the time runs down. By the time we hear the buzzer signalling the end, we've managed to just put the finishing touches on the angel. I'm proud of how it came out. We chose an angel because

Brandon's mom was killed by a drunk driver a few years ago. Her memory lives on in Brandon's heart. She's his angel.

"No matter what happens," I begin as we put our tools down as the judges start to examine each sculpture, "you're getting that scholarship." My voice is low. Only he can hear, but it's something I spoke about to every person in the club. A vote was taken, and everyone unanimously agreed that if Brandon doesn't win, he's getting a scholarship regardless.

"Thank you, sir," Brandon says, getting choked up.

Brandon has come a long way from where he began. He's a success story for us. We turned his life from drugs to something he can be proud of.

After what seems like agonizing hours, Jason picks up the mic again. "It's with great pleasure that I get to announce the winner of this year's contest. With a baby dolphin and its parent, the winner is, Lara Towers with Adrian Sloan!"

We all clap and cheer. I give Brandon a bit of a bump and grin. He turns and hugs me. I smile and hug him back tightly because I feel like he needs it. If he doesn't get anything else this Christmas, at least he'll know he's got friends in this community.

❄❄❄

"What did you wish for?" I ask Jake with a grin as the two of us and Adrian put our wishes up on the Wish Tree at Walker Ranch. Everyone is gathered around the stage as our very own country superstar sings Christmas songs.

"I can't tell you that. It won't come true." Jake kisses my shoulder with an adorable as fuck giggle that does embarrassing things to me.

"I don't even know if I should add my wish. It already came true, so I just said thanks for granting my wish."

I smile at Adrian. "I did the exact same thing."

Jake blinks at the both of us with his mouth slightly open. "Did… you guys put a wish related to our love on there? Dammit! I should've done that." He turns to the tree to find his wish.

"Hey." I grab his wrist. "No. You can't take your wish back."

"It's dumb, though. I wished for a sportsbike like yours so I can ride with you guys."

Adrian raises his eyebrow. "First of all, that's a fucking amazing wish."

"And second, your wish isn't dumb," I finish with a teasing swat to his perfect ass.

He jumps, gives me a sexy look, and grins devilishly. Before I can do anything about the tease, though, Raina appears next to me like she teleported from somewhere.

"Hi, dad! Jaxon says he's ready for you guys on the line to help give out the Christmas dinners. They have a lot of people this year in need."

I nod. "Yeah, I suppose. It's been a fucking insane year."

Raina smiles, but it's sad. "I know I'm not an adult, but… I just think everything going on in the world is stupid. Maybe I should run for Congress so I can whip them all into shape."

Adrian laughs. "I'll back you a thousand percent if you were to run for Congress. And I'd pay extra to see you whip everyone into shape."

I grin. "My little girl. Wanting to beat up grown men and women for being idiots. I love it."

"I get it from you." Raina giggles and skips towards the stage singing *Jingle Bell Rock* along with Lila.

"She definitely gets that stubborn ass attitude from you," Adrian teases. I laugh.

"Also that protective part. She doesn't like people messing with what's hers or what she cares about. Or who," Jake says, shaking his head. He learned the hard way when he jokingly hid her teddy bear. She didn't talk to him all day and made him apologize.

On his knees.

We head over to the area where they're handing out food to people and meet up with Jaxon.

"Hey, man. Where do you want us?" I ask.

"We're expecting around a thousand this year," Jaxon says. "Maybe up to fifteen hundred. We have enough for fifteen hundred, so I hope we don't run out. I have the three of you on the end. We have names on lists. All in alphabetical order. Your group is going to be 'S' through

'Z'. If people come who aren't on the list, write them down in the back. There's blank paper there with the info you'll need."

"Got it. What if you have extras?" I ask.

"Whatever is left, we're donating to the foodbank. We already donated five hundred units, but they told me they have people coming in from smaller, rural areas around here. Still in our county, but too small to have a foodbank of their own. If we don't have anything left, I'm going to go buy another five hundred units."

"Very kind of you, Mr. Walker," Jake says from next to me. He's a little behind me because he's shy around new people.

"Call me, Jaxon, Jake. We're all friends here. Have fun, and thanks for helpin' out!" Jaxon tips his head and walks away to help someone with something else.

"He's really well prepared. Damn," Adrian comments. "He's got signs up. Ropes up to create the lines for each area."

"He's done this every year for quite awhile." I open our binder, surprised to see we have around a couple hundred names. Maybe a few more.

"Merry Christmas, everyone!" Lila says from the stage. "I've just been informed that if you signed up for a family meal, they're all ready to start! Just head on over by the lawn near the driveway, and find your area."

She launches into another song, and I smile. Lila Rose has been the pride of Piper Falls since she was in her teens. We were all proud when she hit it big and started recording for a label in Nashville. She's never forgotten where she came from and still lives here with her husband, Blake. He's a captain with the Piper Falls Fire Department and one of my favorite people.

"Come on, please. Please don't fight me. We'll go home soon," a young woman says. She's practically dragging a sniffling toddler with her while she holds another one on her arm. She looks like she's about to cry.

"What's your name, little one?" Jake asks the toddler, immediately kneeling down.

She hugs her mom's leg. "S-Sara."

"Well, Sara. I'm Jake. Did you have fun today?"

Jake engages Sara in a conversation that has me and Adrian smiling. The young mom smiles gratefully.

"What's your last name, ma'am?" I ask, flipping open the book.

"Smith. My first name is Jannie."

"Alright, Ms. Smith. Let's get you your food and get you off to your car," Adrian says. "Jake and I will give you a hand."

"Oh, thank you so much."

Jake has the little girl laughing by the time they start walking Jannie to her car. I'm already feeling good about helping people.

"Hey, Adam," Brandon says as he walks up to me with his dad. His dad looks rundown and tired.

"Hey, man. What's up?"

"Just here to grab some food. My dad lost his job a few months ago, so it's been a real struggle. That gift card came in real handy to help out with some stuff."

I look from him to his dad after looking up his name. "Alright. I got your food right here." I grab a box for them and a bag out of the cooler. I bring it back and set it on the table.

Brandon's dad clears his throat. "Thanks for, uh. Thanks for giving my son a job. It'll really help us out."

"Yeah, absolutely. And if you need one, let me know. I'm always looking for people. Construction, but we've always got room for people."

He nods and grabs both the box and the bag. Brandon stays behind. "Really, I want to thank you for everything. I was able to get our lights turned back on with that money. And get some groceries."

I chew the inside of my cheek as I think. "Brandon, how much are you guys down?"

"Well, with the utilities and everything, probably around five grand. Not counting food."

I take out my wallet and give him my business card. "Meet me tomorrow at that location. I'll give you an advance on your paycheck. I pay well. We'll set up payments to pay me back. Bring your dad. If he wants a job, I'll give him one on the spot."

"You don't have to do that," Brandon says after a few moments.

"I know. But I want to. You're a good kid. Down on your luck. One day, pay it forward when you have the means. Kindness is always the best policy."

He reaches out to shake my hand. I take it. "Thank you, sir," he says as he lets go and hurries after his dad.

"That was a good thing you did there," Adrian says when he and Jake come back. "We overheard some of that. Mostly about the advance."

"They hit some rough times. We have the means to help. So, I'm giving him an advance on his pay. He can pay it back in installments so we're not taking his whole check."

"I love how kind you are," Jake says, kissing my arm. I kiss his head as we all start handing out more boxes of food.

They say 'Tis the Season when it comes to helping people, but I prefer doing it year round. And now that my life's settled, that's exactly what I plan to do.

Chapter Nineteen

(Christmas Day)

"Oh… my… fuck…" I moan as Adam thrusts into me from underneath. My cock is deep in Adrian's ass as he bounces on it. To anyone looking in, it probably looks like we're playing a game of naked twister on the floor of our bedroom in front of our fireplace, but that's far from what we're doing.

"Holy hell… you feel... so good… stretching my ass," Adrian says between bounces.

"You're so tight around me," I manage to groan out as Adam hits my spot for the millionth time. I'm so close to coming that I keep having to do all I can to hold back. It's not easy because that means squeezing my ass. And when I do that, Adam feels a lot bigger and thicker inside me.

"Damn, baby boy," Adam grunts out, gripping my hips and holding me down on him so each thrust feels like he's hitting my stomach.

Adrian shifts and leans forward as he bounces. It gives me a good view of my dick pumping into his ass. It's one of the sexiest sights ever, and I now understand why Adam and Adrian love the view so much. It makes me impossibly harder.

I feel my ass pulsing around Adam. My cock throbs inside Adrian. He tights around me as he starts stroking himself. We all moan. The sounds of our skin and our wetness smack together, eliciting the most dirty and sexy sounds, making a shiver run down my spine.

"Fuck, I'm gonna come!" I shout. I'm trembling with the effort to hold back.

"Then come. Fill my ass." Adrian looks back at me with a devilish smirk that has jets of come shooting out of me without any effort on my part.

"Ah! Holy fuck!" I shout, gripping whatever I can get my hands on. That happens to be Adam's wrists.

Adam grunts, gripping my hips hard enough to leave marks as he buries himself deep and comes with a roar. I'll never be used to his size. And I'll never be able to get used to feeling like he's coming in my stomach. I don't know how that's possible, but it's the way he always makes it feel.

So good.

So intense.

Every single time.

After we all catch our breath, we make our way to the bathroom to clean up. The shower is big enough to fit all three of us. We often get up to more sexy trouble in there, and today is no different.

After we finish whatever round we're on, I lost count hours ago, I fall against the wall exhausted. I'm satiated in ways I've never felt before.

"You okay, babe?" Adrian asks, rubbing my back.

"Yeah. Just… wow. I've always wanted an all nighter, but damn. That was amazing."

"Speaking of 'wow', I thought we could start cooking dinner and do presents and then get on the game for a bit. We've had so much going on, we haven't been on there much."

I look up at Adam as he starts washing his hair. "I'm positive the guild has fallen apart. Given what Presley has been saying."

"Well, we have our core members. And we all agreed the break was needed. People were leaving for the holidays anyway," Adrian says with a shrug. "Honestly, if we lost everyone but our core group, I don't care. We'll just start over."

"I just want to get on there to see if we can collect some special stuff. Run some quests," Adam says. "And maybe zone out a bit."

"Sounds like a plan to me." I start washing my hair when Adam's done.

Once we're all finished and dressed, we head downstairs to start the turkey and get some prep going. Brandon and his dad will be here for dinner later today. We're going to open presents as soon as Raina is up.

As we all move as a well-oiled machine, I can't help but smile. So much has happened over the past few months, but it's all brought us not only together, but even closer than any of us ever imagined. We've not only become lovers, but we've also become a family. Three dads and a kid.

The thought makes me chuckle to myself as I peel potatoes. I look around the house with excitement for today and what's to come in our future.

For once, our lives will be filled with love and happiness. And like the little bit of snow that's currently blanketing the ground in a pristine white blanket making everything seem shiny and new, it feels like we're starting our lives clean.

I can't wait to share every moment with them.

The End

Piper Falls: Christmas Series

Available Now

Lost For Christmas by Melony Ann
A Cowboys Christmas by Anneke Boshoff
Escape For Christmas by Louise Murchie
Home For Christmas by Lauren L. Moon
Hunted For Christmas by Samantha Michaels
Redemption At Christmas by Claire Davon
A Highland Homestead Christmas by Juliet McKinley
Crazy For Christmas by Maya Black
Mr. Grump's Christmas by Liza Bee
A Grump For Christmas by Airicka Phoenix

Other Books By Melony Ann

The Beautiful Dream Series

Available Now

Loving You
My Love, My Heart
Softening Lyric
Undercover Temptations
Captain Charming
Breaking Boundaries
Crashing Into You
Tactical Inferno
Ravishing Our Queen
Cherished By The Texan
Unveiling Our Passions

Box Sets Available

The Beautiful Dream Series: Box Set: Part 1
The Beautiful Dream Series: Box Set: Part 2

Available Now

The Reluctant Mafia King
Sweet Lies
Billion Dollar Love Story
Be Mine
Protecting Her
Dangerously Forbidden Love
His Heart
Love In The Dark

Box Sets Available

The Crane Family Series

Available Now

Connor's Legacy
Aryan's Alpha
Kade's Redemption

Box Sets Available

The Deimos Trilogy

The Forbidden Temptation Series

Available Now

The Detective's Forbidden Temptation
The Running Back's Forbidden Temptation
The Prez's Forbidden Temptation
The Coach's Forbidden Temptation
The Tight End's Forbidden Temptation

The Lucinio Family Series

Available Now

Rising From The Ashes
The Player's Rebel
Encrypting My Heart
Fighting My Fate
Phoenix Rising
Defending Her Honor

Snowed In Trilogy

Available Now

Snowed In For Christmas
Snowed In With The Stalker
Snowed In With My Best Friend

Multi Author Series

Piper Falls: Firehouse 49

Available Now

Ignite My Fire by Melony Ann
Regain My Fire by Kindra White
Playing With My Fire by D.L. Howe
Fight My Fire by Darley Collins
Against My Fire by Anneke Boshoff
Relight My Fire by Louise Murchie
Harness My Fire by Ayana Lisbet
Quench My Fire by Havana Wilder

Available Now

Embracing My Duty by Melony Ann
Torn By My Duty by Kayla Baker
Against My Duty by Anneke Boshoff
Defying My Duty by D.L. Howe
Leave Of My Duty by Nikki A. Lamers
Fulfilling My Duty by Havana Wilder
Following My Duty by Louise Murchie
Replete In My Duty by Stacy Kristen
Accepting My Duty by Darley Collins

Let's Be Friends

Follow me on

Bluesky

Bookbub

Facebook

Goodreads

Instagram

Patreon
Subscribe today and get an exclusive book!

Threads

Tik Tok

X

Visit my website
www.melonyannauthor.com

Subscribe to my newsletter and get a FREE never-seen-before NOVELLA just for subscribers!
https://www.melonyannauthor.com/exclusive-content

Join my Facebook Reader Group!
Melony Ann's Sizzling Book Nook

The official Playlist on Spotify

Acknowledgements

To my loves.

To my friends.

To my team.

To the Bookstagram Community.

To my family.

To all of those who believe in me and support me.

To all of those who don't.

Cover by: LC Designs

About Melony Ann

Melony Ann began writing short stories and poetry as a child. She continued honing her craft over the years until she took the plunge and began publishing her work, despite having severe anxiety.

Melony is an award winning author, winning a coveted Firebird Award, and writes contemporary romance stories that are full of suspense and a lot of steam.

When she isn't writing, she is loving her family and working to make her life something she deserves.

Melony believes that if her writing can inspire just one person, then all of her hard work is worth it.

Her hope is that her writing allows each and every one of her readers to escape for a little while. To dive into a different world one book at a time.

www.ingramcontent.com/pod-product-compliance
Lightning Source LLC
LaVergne TN
LVHW010916110826
845149LV00013B/2383

* 9 7 8 1 9 6 1 9 6 6 8 3 3 *